THE TREEHOUSE FUN BOOK

ANDY GRIFFITHS
JILL GRIFFITHS
and TERRY DENTON

FEIWEL AND FRIENDS

Feiwel and Friends • New York

A Feiwel and Friends Book
An Imprint of Macmillan

Printed in the United States of America by R. R. Donnelley & Sons Company, Harrisonburg, Virginia. For information, address Feiwel and Friends, 175 Fifth Avenue, New York, N.Y. 10010.

Our books may be purchased in bulk for promotional, educational, or business use. Please contact your local bookseller or the Macmillan Corporate and Premium Sales Department at (800) 221-7945 ext. 5442 or by e-mail at MacmillanSpecialMarkets@macmillan.com.

ISBN 978-1-250-11775-5

Feiwel and Friends logo designed by Filomena Tuosto

Originally published in Australia in 2016 by Pan Macmillan Australia Pty Ltd

First published in the United States by Feiwel and Friends, an imprint of Macmillan

First U.S. Edition—2016

10 9 8 7 6 5 4 3 2 1

mackids.com

Grand opening!
Treehouse Fun Book!
Come one, come all!
Fun for all ages!

Hi, I'm Andy.
book
Andy

Hi, I'm Terry.
pencil
Terry

Hi, I'm Jill.
And I'm Silky.
Jill
Silky

I like to write.
I like to draw.

I like animals. I also like solving problems and doing puzzles.
I like cat food, cuddles, cats on TV, and Jill.

DRAW YOURSELF

Now it's your turn. Draw yourself and write your name.

Hi, I'm VIV

Draw your pet, too, if you have one. If you don't, you could draw one you would like to have.

DRAW SOMETHING YOU LIKE

Draw something you like or something you like to do.

mr B

I like to Backe, play.

DRAW SOMETHING YOU DON'T LIKE

Draw something you don't like or something you don't like to do.

yuc
I don't like
Brok ley

Terry and I live in a treehouse.
Hee, haw!
QUICK SAND

I live in a house full of animals.
BAA!
SNAP!
MOO

DRAW WHERE YOU LIVE

Draw where you live.
Who lives there with you? Draw them.
Draw any animals that live there, too.

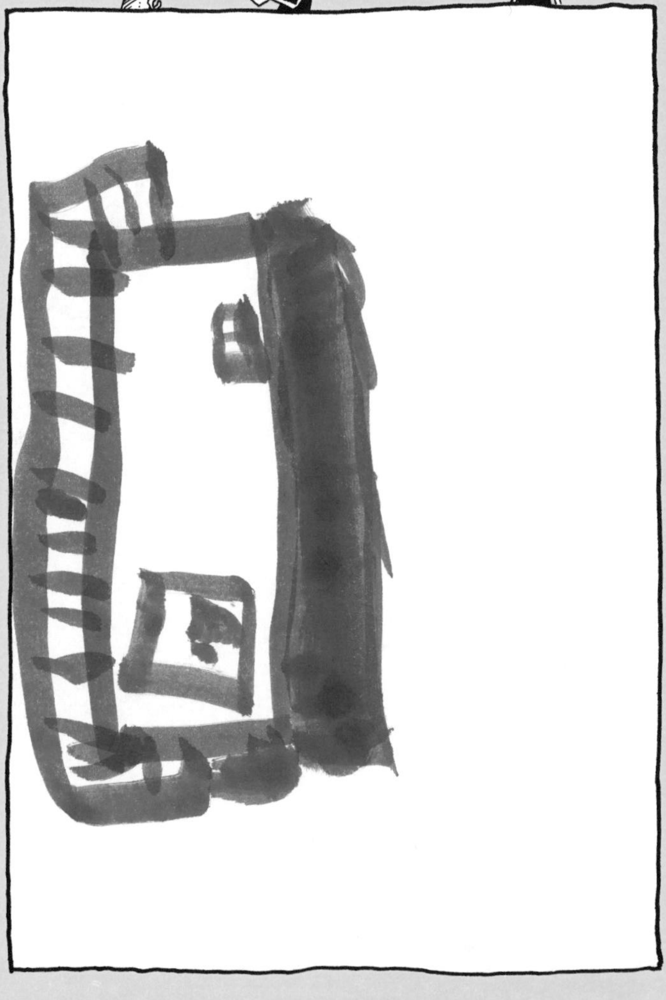

LIST NEW TREEHOUSE LEVELS

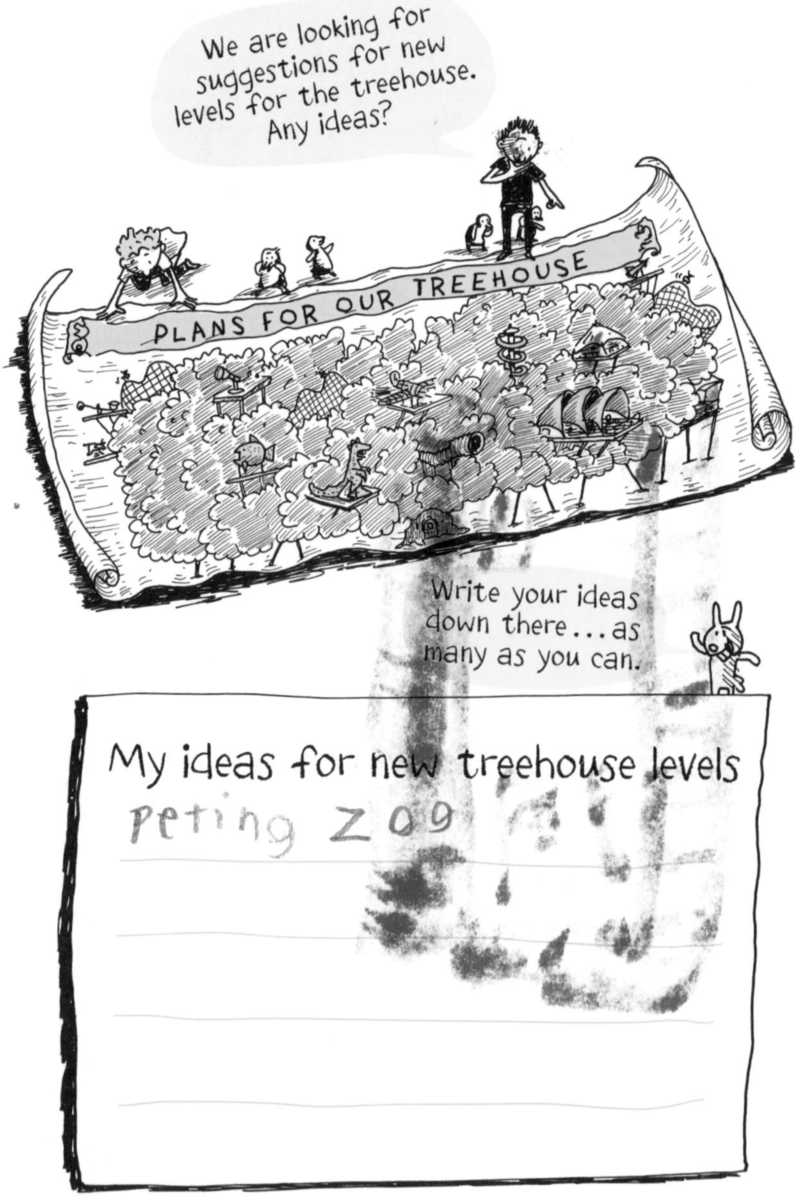
We are looking for suggestions for new levels for the treehouse. Any ideas?
PLANS FOR OUR TREEHOUSE
Write your ideas down there . . . as many as you can.

My ideas for new treehouse levels

peting Zo9

Write your ideas up there.

DRAW NEW TREEHOUSE LEVELS

Choose two levels from your list and draw them.
You can add labels, too. I LOVE labels.

Beach

PLAN YOUR TREEHOUSE VISIT

There is a lot of fun stuff to do in our treehouse. Here are 13 things you can do. What order—from 1 to 13—would you do them in?

☐ comic reading

PINGU

☐ pillow fighting

☐ marshmallow eating

Uh, oh.
Hee, hee.
BOOM

☐ inventing

Weeee!
SPLAT!

☐ swinging

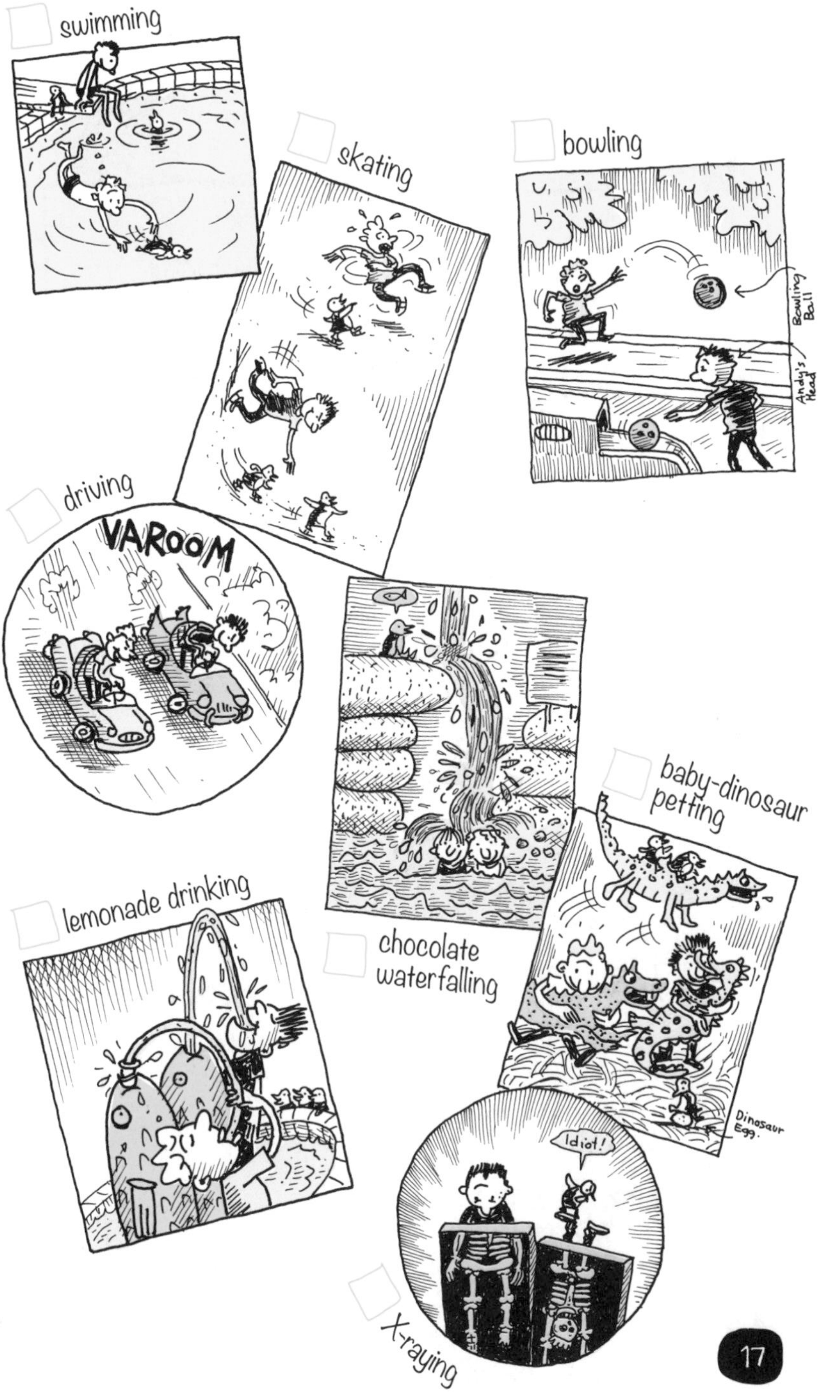
swimming
skating
bowling
Bowling Ball
Andy's Head
driving
VAROOM
chocolate waterfalling
baby-dinosaur petting
Dinosaur Egg.
lemonade drinking
Idiot!
X-raying

Terry is really busy. Look at his TO-DO list.
You might need to turn the book upside down.
1. Do have pillow fight with Andy.
2. Do prepare birthday party for sharks.
3. Do practice golf swing.
4. Do eat at least 100 marshmallows.
5. Do polish the parrot.
6. Do cut toenails.
7. Do hit Andy with bowling ball.
8. Do eat all the chocolates in the treehouse.
9. Do tickle the parrot.
10. Do sleep on the roof.

WRITE YOUR TO-DO LIST

Write your list down there.

What's on **your** TO-DO list?

Do Go to DiSNY world

Do

Do

Doo-doo!
Doo-doo!

Terry also has a really long TO-DON'T list.
5. Don't fall out of the treehouse.
6. Don't fall into man-eating-shark tank.
7. Don't make Andy cry.
8. Don't eat the man-eating sharks.
9. Don't set fire to my head.
10. Don't wash.
11. Don't stand under falling piano.
12. Don't wash my undies.
13. Don't wash Andy's undies.
14. Dont
undies.
15. Do
anything
else.
16. Do
or his
leg.
Flie inside
Big Nose!!
cookies or
cake.
fireans

WRITE YOUR TO-DON'T LIST

Write your list down there.

What's on **your** TO-DON'T list?
Don't
Don't
Don't

Don't-don't!
That's not funny.

ICE CREAM TIME

Let's go get an ice cream.
Great idea, Andy!
Oh no! Some of the ice cream flavors are missing!
Professor Stupido must have un-invented them.
Let's get the reader to invent some new ones.
Great idea, Jill!

DRAW NEW ICE CREAM FLAVORS

Draw the new flavors and write what each one is.
CHERRY
BLUEBERRY BURST
GOLDFISH SURPRISE
FLYING MONKEY
Goldfish surprise is my favorite.
Flying monkey is better!
Flying monkey?!

FLYING TIME

I'm flying in my jet-powered office chair.
Flying horse
That's amazing!
Amazed bird
EEEEK!!

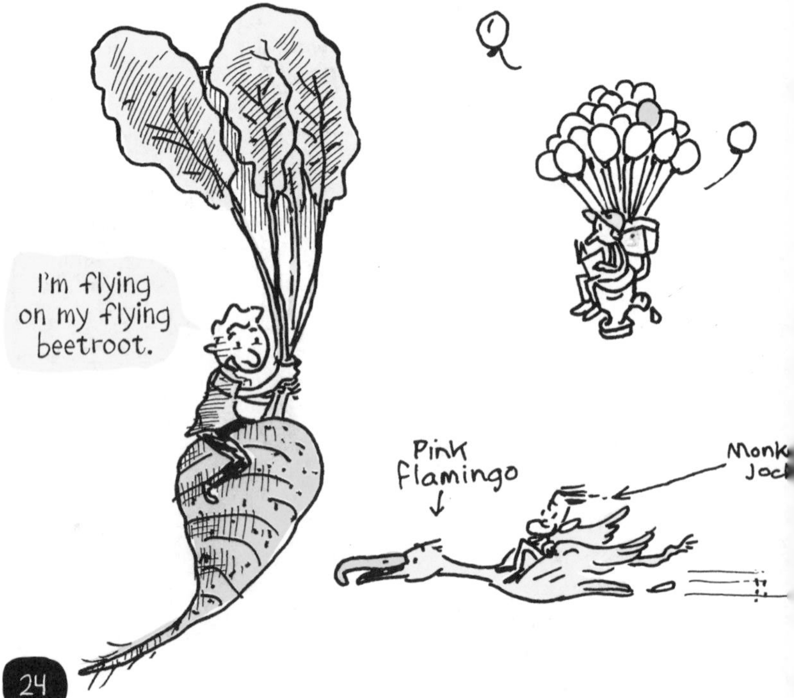
I'm flying on my flying beetroot.
Pink flamingo
Monk
Joc

I'm flying in my flying-cat sleigh.
What are you going to fly in—or on? Draw it.
pug pug

DOT-TO-DOT FUN

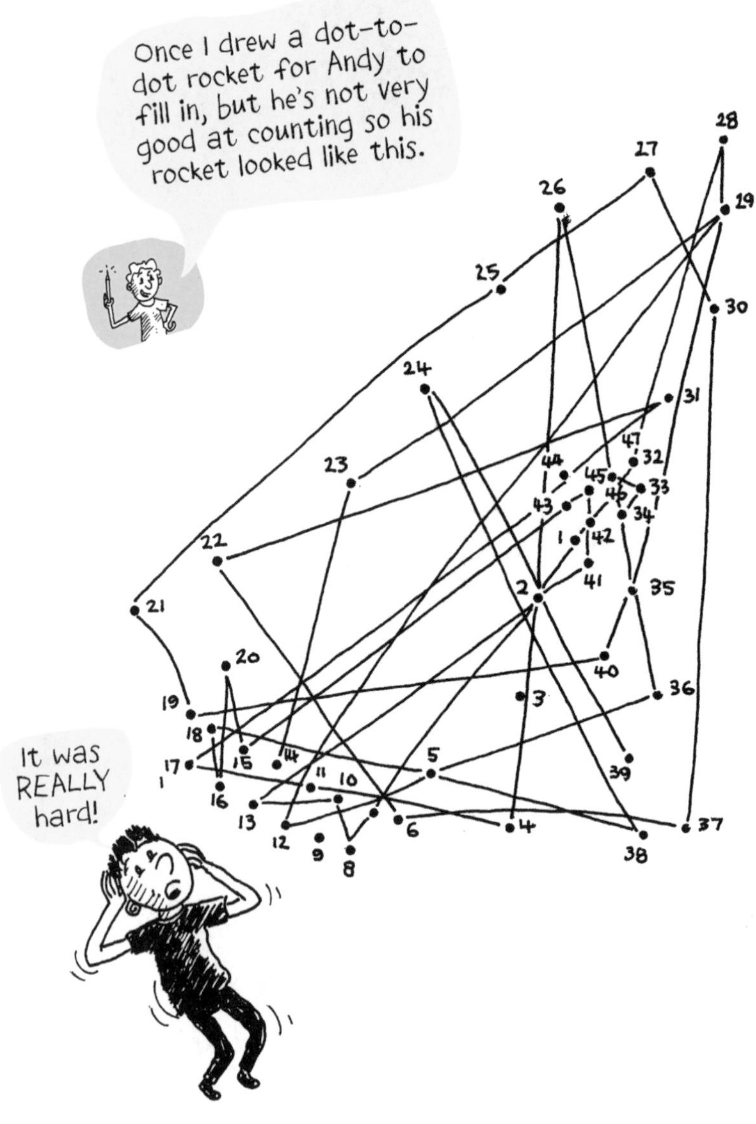
Once I drew a dot-to-dot rocket for Andy to fill in, but he's not very good at counting so his rocket looked like this.
It was REALLY hard!

See if you can join the dots to make a better dot-to-dot rocket than Andy.
Good luck! It's not easy.
I'll do it!

COUNT US DOWN

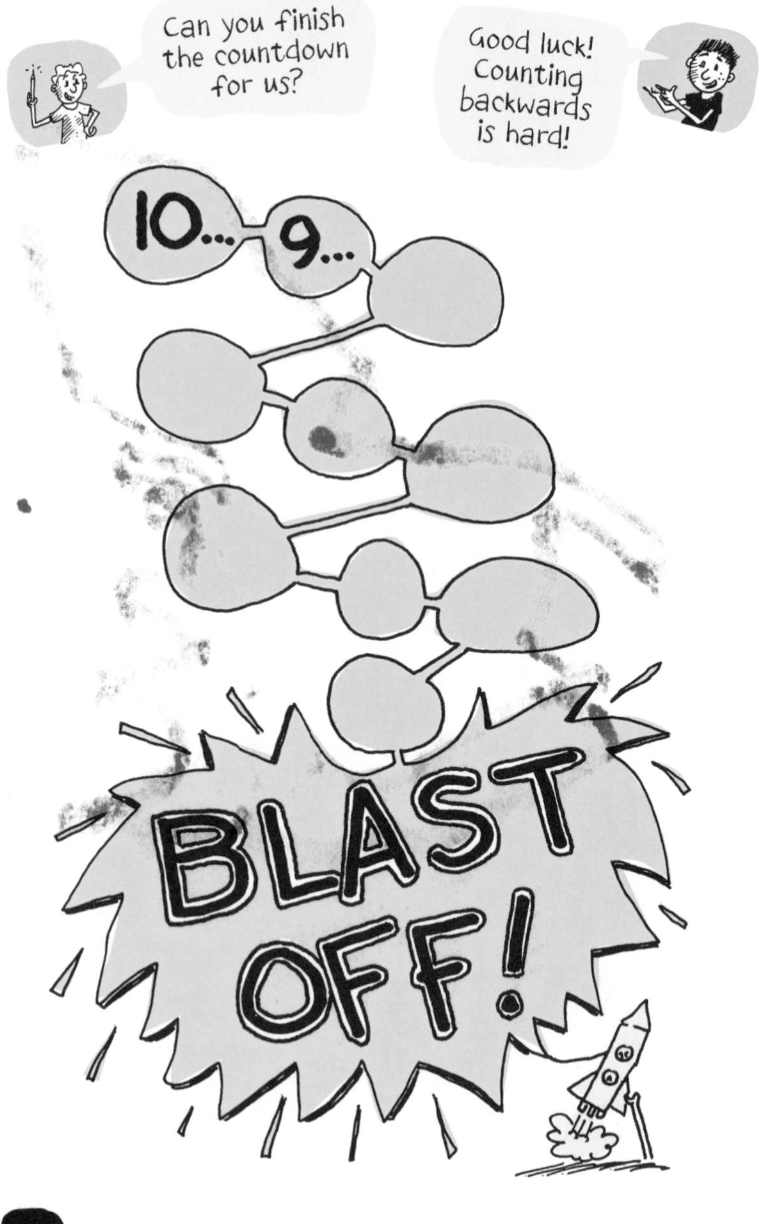
Can you finish the countdown for us?
Good luck! Counting backwards is hard!
10...
9...
BLAST OFF!

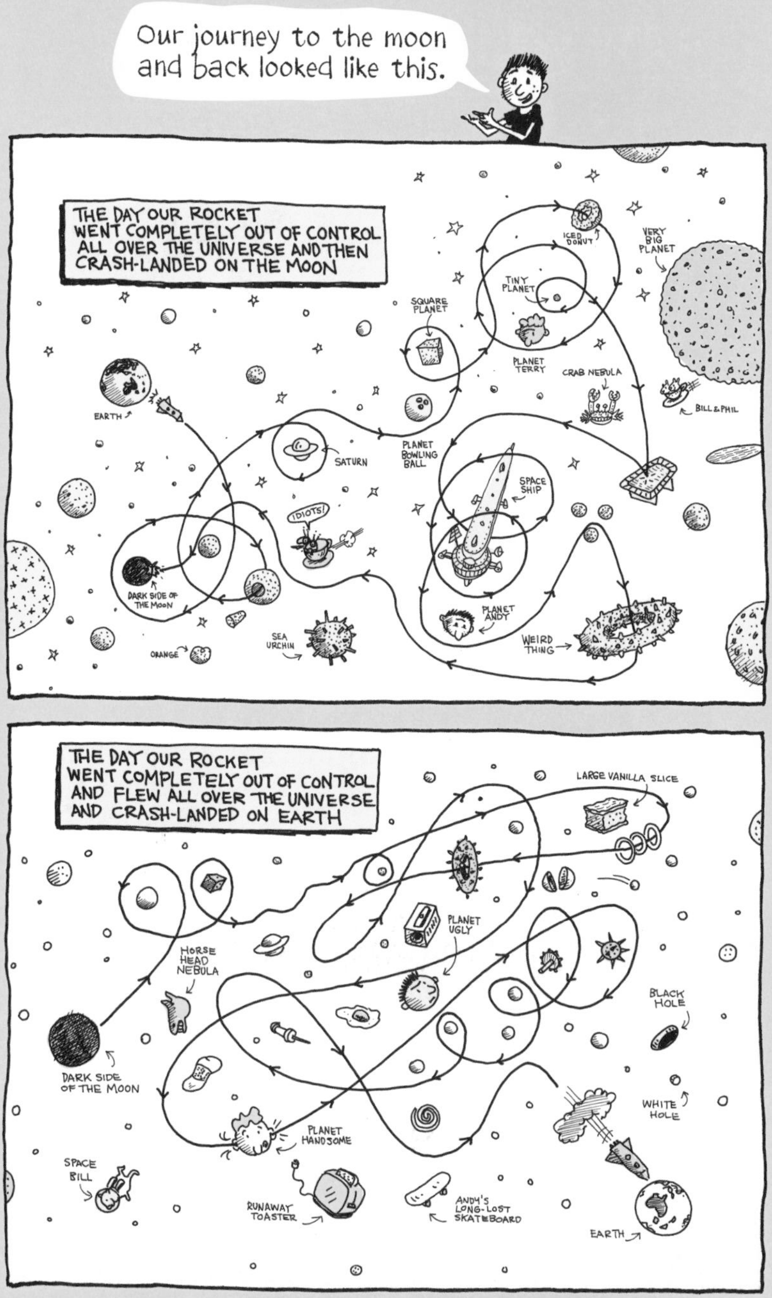

Our journey to the moon and back looked like this.
THE DAY OUR ROCKET WENT COMPLETELY OUT OF CONTROL ALL OVER THE UNIVERSE AND THEN CRASH-LANDED ON THE MOON
ICED DONUT
VERY BIG PLANET
TINY PLANET
SQUARE PLANET
PLANET TERRY
CRAB NEBULA
EARTH
BILL & PHIL
SATURN
PLANET BOWLING BALL
SPACE SHIP
IDIOTS!
DARK SIDE OF THE MOON
PLANET ANDY
SEA URCHIN
WEIRD THING
ORANGE
THE DAY OUR ROCKET WENT COMPLETELY OUT OF CONTROL AND FLEW ALL OVER THE UNIVERSE AND CRASH-LANDED ON EARTH
LARGE VANILLA SLICE
PLANET UGLY
HORSE HEAD NEBULA
BLACK HOLE
DARK SIDE OF THE MOON
WHITE HOLE
PLANET HANDSOME
SPACE BILL
RUNAWAY TOASTER
ANDY'S LONG-LOST SKATEBOARD
EARTH

DRAW YOUR SPACE JOURNEY

What does your space journey look like? Where did you go? What did you fly past? Did you crash?

SPOT THE DIFFERENCE

Can you spot 13 differences between these pictures?

Answers are on page 152.

DRAW OUR SHARKS

Oh no! Professor Stupido has un-invented our man-eating sharks.
Draw them back for us.

UN-INVENT SOMETHING

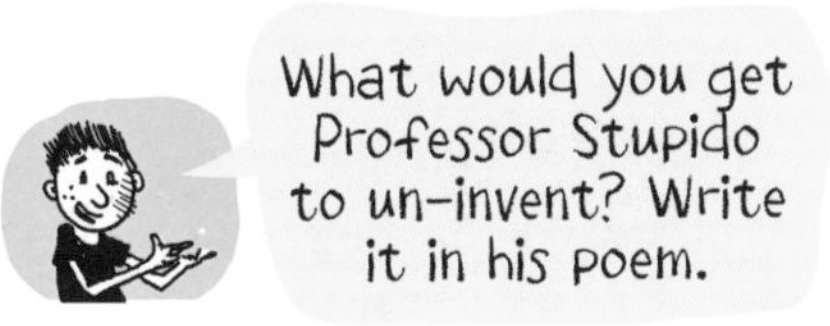
What would you get Professor Stupido to un-invent? Write it in his poem.

And draw it, too.

Roses are red,
Violets are blue.
I don't like
____
So I un-invent you.

BARKY TIME

Yay! My favorite show is on. Barky the Barking Dog!
Oh no, not Barky! He's boring!
BARKY AND THE BIG HOLE
BARK
BARK
BARK
BARK
YAWN!
Z
I hate Barky.
I love Tweety the Tweeting Bird.

What is Barky barking at now? Draw it.
BARK
BARK

BARK

BARK

BARK

BARK

Fill in the speech bubbles to show what you think Barky is REALLY saying when he barks.
Hello, hello! Is there anybody down there?

SPOT THE DIFFERENCE

Can you spot 13 differences between these pictures?
Mommy, those two don't look like real monkeys.
Shhh! Don't talk so loud. You'll hurt their feelings.
I hate bananas.
Shut up and eat.

Answers are on page 153.
Mommy, those two don't look like real monkeys.
Shhh! Don't talk so loud. You'll hurt their feelings.
I love bananas.
Shut up and eat.

Our Maze of Doom is pretty dangerous. I think we need some more warning signs. Write some in the blank signs the penguins are holding.
MAZE OF DOOM
Help!
I'm lost!
Penguin bros... where are you?
ARE YOU CRAZY!
HAZARD
ENTER AT OWN RISK
CERTAIN DEATH AHEAD

WRITE SOME WARNING SIGNS

ESCAPE THE MAZE OF DOOM

(IF YOU CAN!)

Can you find your way out of this maze or are you doomed?
The answer is on page 154.
YOU ARE HERE

ENLARGING TIME

Would you like something enlarged? Draw it under my enlarging ray.

Draw it up there.

13-STORY TREEHOUSE WORD SEARCH

When you have finished there should be 13 letters left over that spell out something to do with the story.

Answers are on page 155.

WORD LIST

BANANA
BATHROOM
BOWLING
CATAPULT
CHAOS
EGGS
KITCHEN
LABORATORY
MONKEY
NOISE
PAWS
SEA MONKEYS
SWINGING
VINES

S	E	A	M	O	N	K	E	Y	S
C	G	A	N	A	N	A	B	R	W
A	N	S	M	O	O	B	N	O	I
T	I	N	G	K	I	A	V	T	N
A	L	E	S	G	S	T	I	A	G
P	W	H	W	E	E	H	N	R	I
U	O	C	A	Y	M	R	E	O	N
L	B	T	P	A	D	O	S	B	G
T	N	I	C	H	A	O	S	A	E
Y	E	K	N	O	M	M	S	L	S

SOLUTION: _ _ _ _ _ _ _   _ _ _ _ _ _ _ _

COLOR IN JILL'S HOUSE

BAA!
SNAP!
MOO

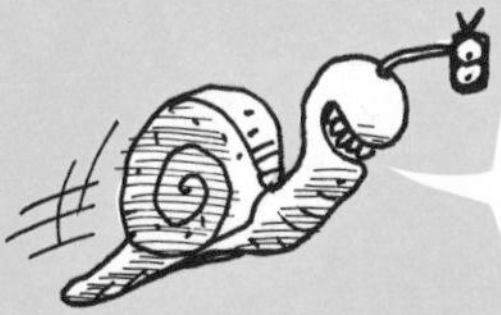
Color in the picture Ninja-style (slowly).

PIZZA TIME

OLIVE OIL
CUSTARD
Tomato Paste
OLIVE PIECES
Over here!
ANCHOVIES
CHEESE GUN
SQUID
FROGS LEGS
NAILS
CLAMS
CACTUS
SNAILS
SPIDERS
Let's make a pizza.

DRAW YOUR OWN PIZZA

Draw your toppings.
What are you going to put on yours?
HAIR
SALAMI
HOT SALAMI
SUPER-HOT SALAMI
CHILIES
SHRIMP
PEPPERS
CHOC CHIPS
SAUSAGE
EGGS
Pizza dough

ANIMAL PIZZAS

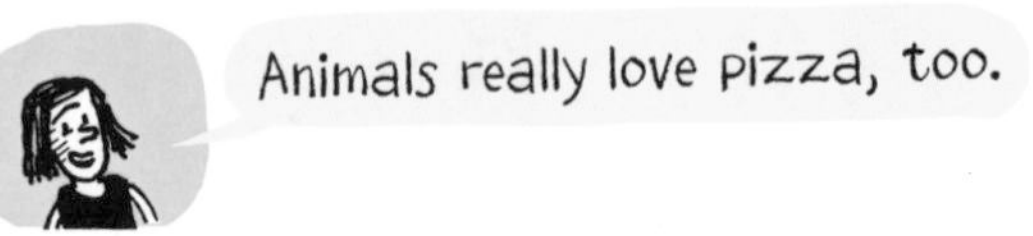
Animals really love pizza, too.

Four fish pizzas, please... with extra fish.
Hee. Hee. Hee.

I said "extra carrot"... don't you people ever listen?

I'd like to order a Hawaiian pizza...

What pizza do you think these animals would order?

26-STORY TREEHOUSE WORD SEARCH

W	O	O	D	E	N	H	E	A	D
I	T	O	I	D	U	T	S	L	U
C	A	L	O	O	P	C	N	O	M
E	T	S	L	L	U	A	R	Z	U
C	T	E	S	U	C	P	H	N	D
R	O	T	K	E	B	T	Y	O	F
E	O	A	A	Z	K	U	M	G	I
A	Y	R	T	A	P	R	E	R	G
M	I	I	E	M	R	E	A	O	H
T	S	P	L	A	T	D	E	G	T

WORD LIST

BULL
CAPTURED
GORGONZOLA
ICE CREAM
MAZE
MUD FIGHT
PIRATES
POOL
SKATE
SPLAT
STUDIO
TATTOO
RHYME
WOODENHEAD

When you have finished there should be 13 letters left over that spell out something to do with the story.

Answers are on page 156.

SOLUTION: _ _ _ _ _ _ _ _ _ _   _ _ _ _ _ _ _ _

COLOR IN THE SHARK TANK

Color in the sharky picture.

Look out, Terry! Behind you!!
Shh! Don't interrupt me. I'm trying to feed the sharks.

DRAWING TIME

I've drawn a worm.
It looks like this.
Yum!
Yum!
T

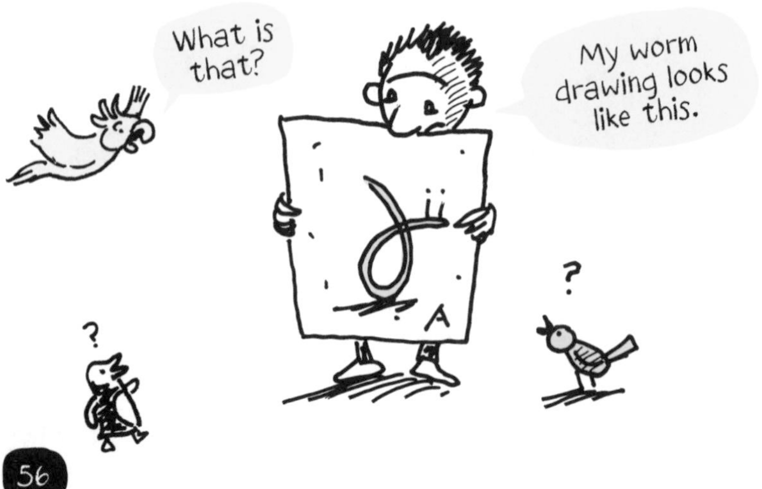
What is
that?
My worm
drawing looks
like this.
?
?
A

DRAW A WORM

Now it's your turn.

Draw your
worm up there.

Now let's draw a banana.
Mine looks like this.
A
Wow, my picture is so good it even tastes like a banana.

DRAW A BANANA

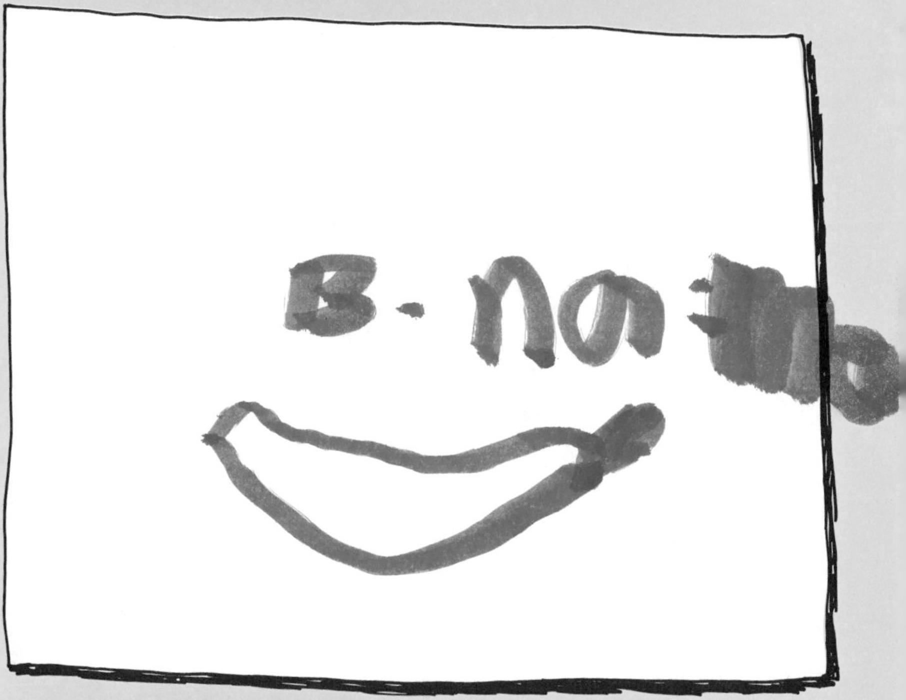
B · na

BA·NA·NA
BA·NA·NA

COLOR IN CHEESELAND

You'll need lots of yellow.

CHEESE
CHEESE FONDUE
CHEESELAND
CHEESELAND
CHEESE SLICES

39-STORY TREEHOUSE WORD SEARCH

When you have finished there should be 12 letters left over that spell out something to do with the story.

WORD LIST

ANDY
BEETROOT
CHOCOLATE
MOON
ROCKET
SILKY
SPOONCIL
STUPIDO
TERRY
TRAMPOLINE
UNINVENT
VOLCANO
WATERFALL

Answers are on page 157.

T	R	A	M	P	O	L	I	N	E
W	E	T	A	L	O	C	O	H	C
A	V	T	O	O	R	T	E	E	B
T	O	S	P	O	O	N	C	I	L
E	L	M	S	L	A	P	A	Y	R
R	C	O	S	L	A	P	N	K	O
F	A	O	S	L	A	P	D	L	C
A	N	N	T	E	R	R	Y	I	K
L	O	D	I	P	U	T	S	S	E
L	U	N	I	N	V	E	N	T	T

SOLUTION: _ _ _ _   _ _ _ _ _   _ _ _ _ _

TATTOO TIME

We're getting tattoos from our Automatic Tattoo Machine.
LOVE
HATE
I ♡ Penguins
A·T·M

DESIGN YOUR OWN TATTOO

What would you like the ATM to tattoo on you? Draw it.

cat
Dog

SPOT THE DIFFERENCE

Can you spot 13 differences between these pictures?
BARKY, THE BARKING DOG AT THE BEACH

Answers are on page 158.

BARKY, THE BARKING DOG AT THE BEACH

SUPERFINGER TIME

Terry and I invented a character called Superfinger.

Once upon a time there was a finger. But it was no ordinary finger . . . it was a Superfinger!

Superfinger solves problems that need finger-based solutions—he can help you tie a bow, point you in the right direction, and help you clear a blocked nose. Any time you need an extra finger, Superfinger is there!

CREATE A SUPERHERO

Draw your own superhero.

THE ADVENTURES OF
SUPER Girl

What can your superhero do?

Ice

Fire

water

REMEMBERING TIME

Draw yourself in the Remembering Booth.

I REMEMBER ...

Write down some stuff you remember.

A fun holiday I had was evrthing

A time I was embarrassed was I Fartin clas

A funny thing that happened to me was Idk

I've orgotten hat I've rgotten.

A time I was really scared was Idk

TREEHOUSE TRIVIA

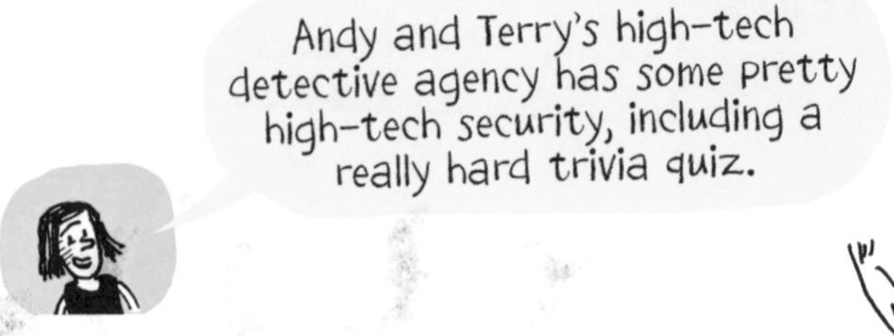
Andy and Terry's high-tech detective agency has some pretty high-tech security, including a really hard trivia quiz.

Mmm... that is REALLY hard.

What are the names of the main characters in the Treehouse series?

It's you!
And you!

How many of these trivia questions can you answer?

1. What is the name of the sea monster Terry fell in love with?

2. What is the worst job Andy and Terry ever had?

3. What is Terry's favorite TV show?

4. What color did Terry paint Silky?

5. What is the name of Andy and Terry's publisher?

6. What is the name of the pirate who captured Andy, Terry, and me?

7. How many flavors of ice cream are there in Edward Scooperhands' ice-cream parlor?

Answers are on page 159.

MISSING PET POSTER

When Silky went missing
I made this poster.
MISSING CAT!
SiLKY
she looks like this
cute little ears
beautiful green eyes
darling whiskers
very soft white fur
Likes: cat food, cuddles, cats on TV
Dislikes: dogs, water, fleas, locked cat flaps
BIG REWARD!! call JILL

Make your own missing pet poster. It could be for a pet you have or a made-up one.

MISSING PET!

Likes:

Dislikes:

BIG REWARD!!

SPOT THE DIFFERENCE

Can you spot 13 differences between these pictures?
THE BIG FAT COW THAT GOES KAPOW!
Z
Z
Z

Answers are on page 160.

52-STORY TREEHOUSE WORD SEARCH

When you have finished there should be 13 letters left over that spell out something to do with the story.

Answers are on page 161.

WORD LIST

ANDY
BIG
BUTTERFLY
DETECTIVES
DISGUISE
EGGPLANT
NINJA
NOSE
PATTY
POTATO
PRINCE
REMEMBER
SNAILS
TERRY

D	E	T	E	C	T	I	V	E	S
E	P	E	C	N	I	R	P	Y	E
G	O	N	B	I	G	D	A	L	R
G	T	S	O	T	V	I	P	F	E
P	A	N	N	S	E	S	A	R	M
L	T	A	I	Y	E	G	T	E	E
A	O	I	N	D	G	U	T	T	M
N	E	L	J	N	T	I	Y	T	B
T	A	S	A	A	B	S	L	U	E
E	T	E	R	R	Y	E	S	B	R

SOLUTION: _ _ _   _ _ _ _ _ _ _ _ _ _

VEGETABLE COLORING TIME

Color in all the lovely vegetables.

MIXED-UP ANIMALS

Yellow
I love animals, especially mixed-up ones, like catnaries and frogpotamuses.
You can talk! You're a mutant spider!
I don't like frogpotamuses– they're gross.

Mix two animals together to create a new one.
+
husky
=

PET MAKEOVER TIME

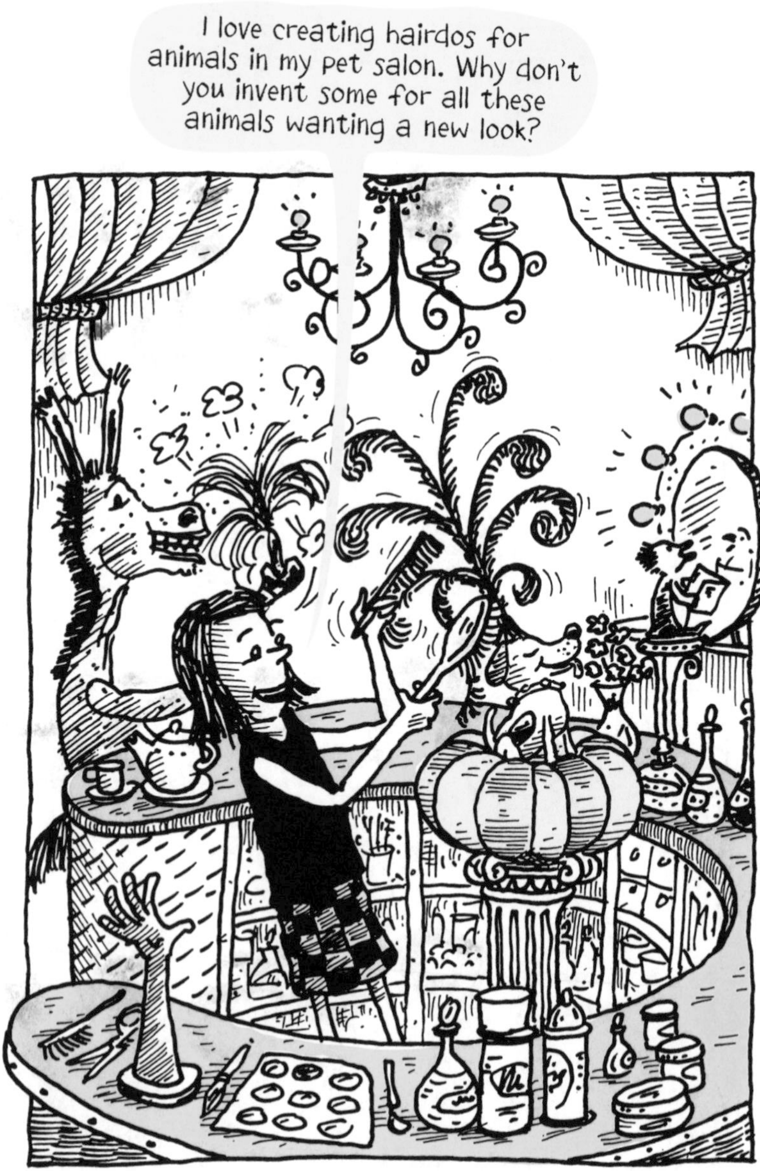
I love creating hairdos for animals in my pet salon. Why don't you invent some for all these animals wanting a new look?

BARK!
Draw me some hair.
BARK!

HAIR-DO!
HAIR-DO!

ROAR!
DRAW ME SOME
HAIR! NOW!

I'm not sure what I want. You choose.
Me first! Do me first!
Ssssomething sssimple, pleassse.
I like curls.

I'm ready for a big change. And I mean BIG!

I need a new look!

Make me pretty.

I feel a change coming on.

Me want hairdo... and ears!

SPOT THE DIFFERENCE

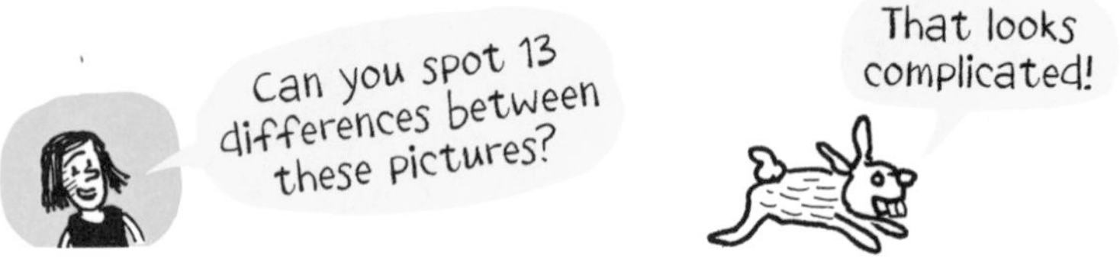
Can you spot 13 differences between these pictures?
That looks complicated!

FRUIT-AND-VEGETABLE-BASED TRANSPORT OPTIONS
CRUISING CARROT
FLYING BEETROOT
FLOATING PEACH
HIGH-SPEED WATERMELON
SINKING STRAWBERRY
ROCKET-PROPELLED EGGPLANT
COIN RETURN
10c

Answers are on page 162.

10¢
FRUIT-AND-VEGETABLE-BASED TRANSPORT OPTIONS
CRUISING CARROT
FLYING BEETROOT
FLOATING CARROT
HIGH-SPEED WATERMELON
SINKING STRAWBERRY
ROCKET-PROPELLED EGGPLANT
COIN RETURN

EXPLODING TIME

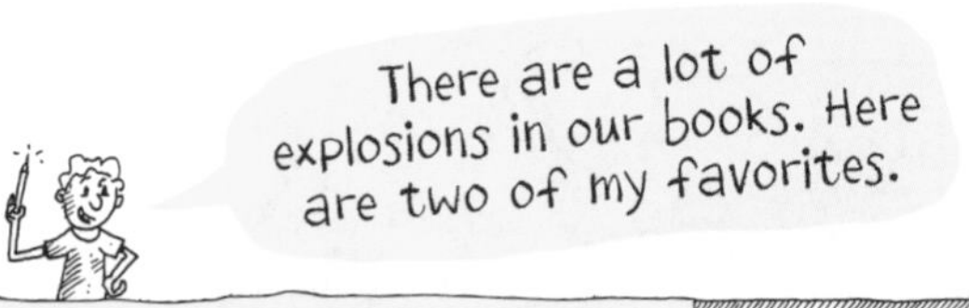
There are a lot of explosions in our books. Here are two of my favorites.

THE DAY GORGONZOLA EXPLODED
KABLAM!

THE DAY THE BIGNOSEASAUR EXPLODED

DRAW AN EXPLOSION

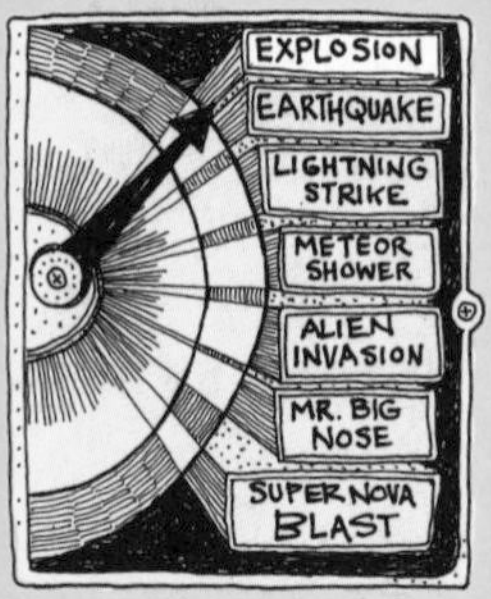
EXPLOSION
EARTHQUAKE
LIGHTNING STRIKE
METEOR SHOWER
ALIEN INVASION
MR. BIG NOSE
SUPERNOVA BLAST

I've set the disaster dial to EXPLOSION so now it's your turn to draw one.

Bom

ANIMAL SCRAMBLES

My animals' names are all mixed up. Can you fix them?

RM EEH WAH

____

EMO

____

SLIYK

____

Answers are on page 163.

LRARY

BLLI & PILH

TAP

SCREECHY COLOR IN

Color in the screechy picture.
SCREECH!!

65-STORY TREEHOUSE WORD SEARCH

When you have finished there should be eight letters left over that spell out something to do with the story.

Answers are on page 164.

WORD LIST

ANTS
ASPS
BIN
BUBBLE WRAP
CLONING

CRAB
EGYPT
FIRE
INSPECTOR

OWLS
PERMIT
POND SCUM
RAMPS

SELFIE
SUPER BW
TIME TRAVEL
TREE NN

B	G	S	B	T	P	Y	G	E	L
U	N	U	A	S	B	I	N	P	E
B	I	P	R	N	E	R	I	F	V
B	N	E	C	O	T	L	O	P	A
L	O	R	P	S	O	S	F	O	R
E	L	B	L	P	E	R	M	I	T
W	C	W	T	R	E	E	N	N	E
R	O	T	C	E	P	S	N	I	M
A	S	P	S	S	P	M	A	R	I
P	O	N	D	S	C	U	M	P	T

SOLUTION: _ _ _ _   _ _ _ _

FIND THE ODD ONE OUT

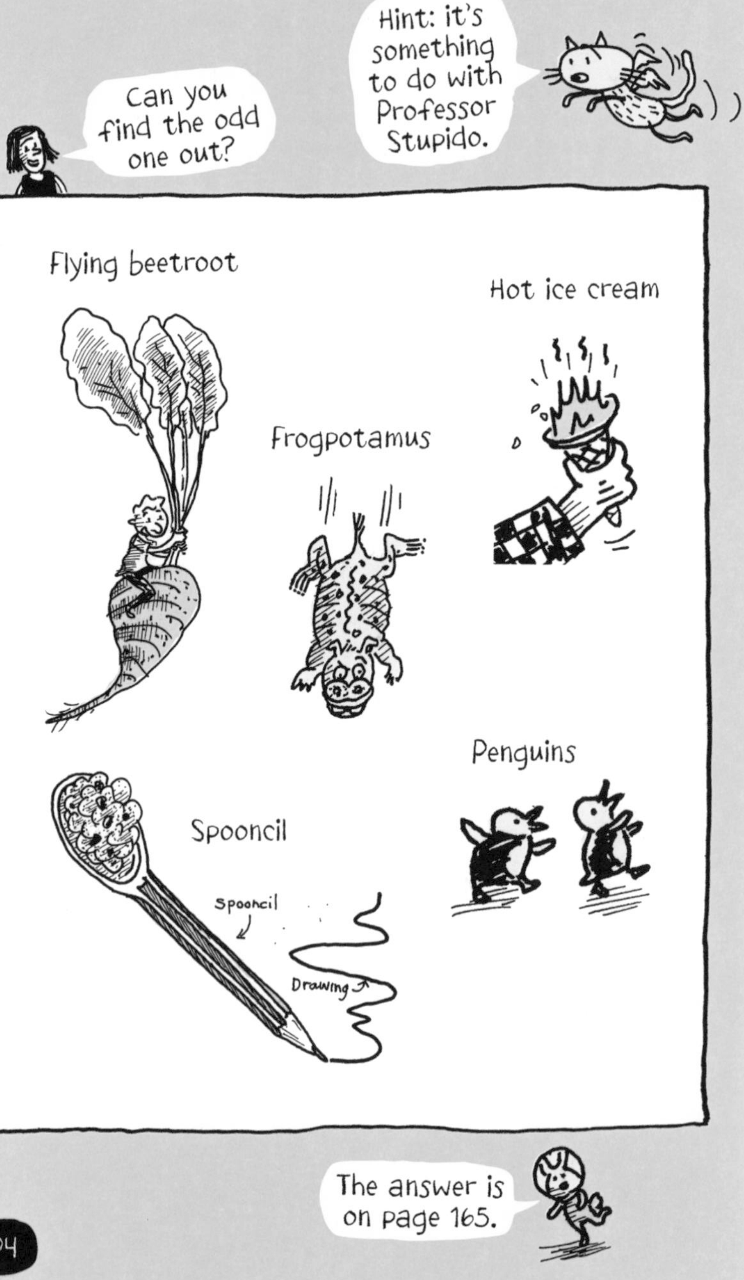
Can you find the odd one out?
Hint: it's something to do with Professor Stupido.
Flying beetroot
Hot ice cream
Frogpotamus
Penguins
Spooncil
spooncil
Drawing
The answer is on page 165.

SOUND EFFECTS FUN

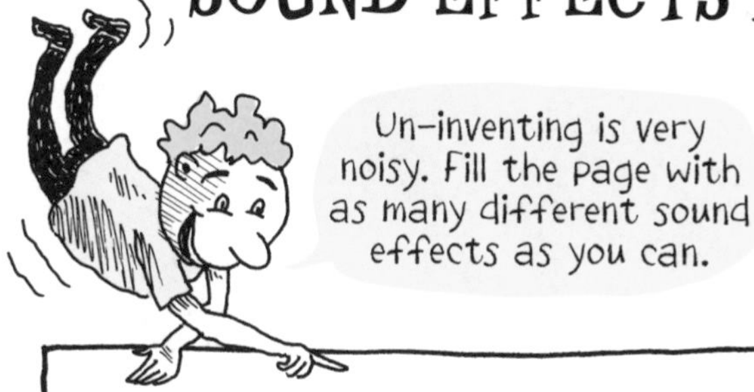
Un-inventing is very noisy. Fill the page with as many different sound effects as you can.

BLEEP!

BLAM!
BLOOT!
BLAM!
BLING!
BLOOT!
BLOOT!
BLING!
BLAM!
BLAM!
BLING!
BLOOT!
BLOOT!
BLING!
BLAM!
BLAM!
BLOOT!
BLING!

VEGETABLE DISGUISE TIME

We need to disguise ourselves as vegetables, so we need some vegetable costumes . . . fast!
Can you draw them for us?
I feel like a pea!

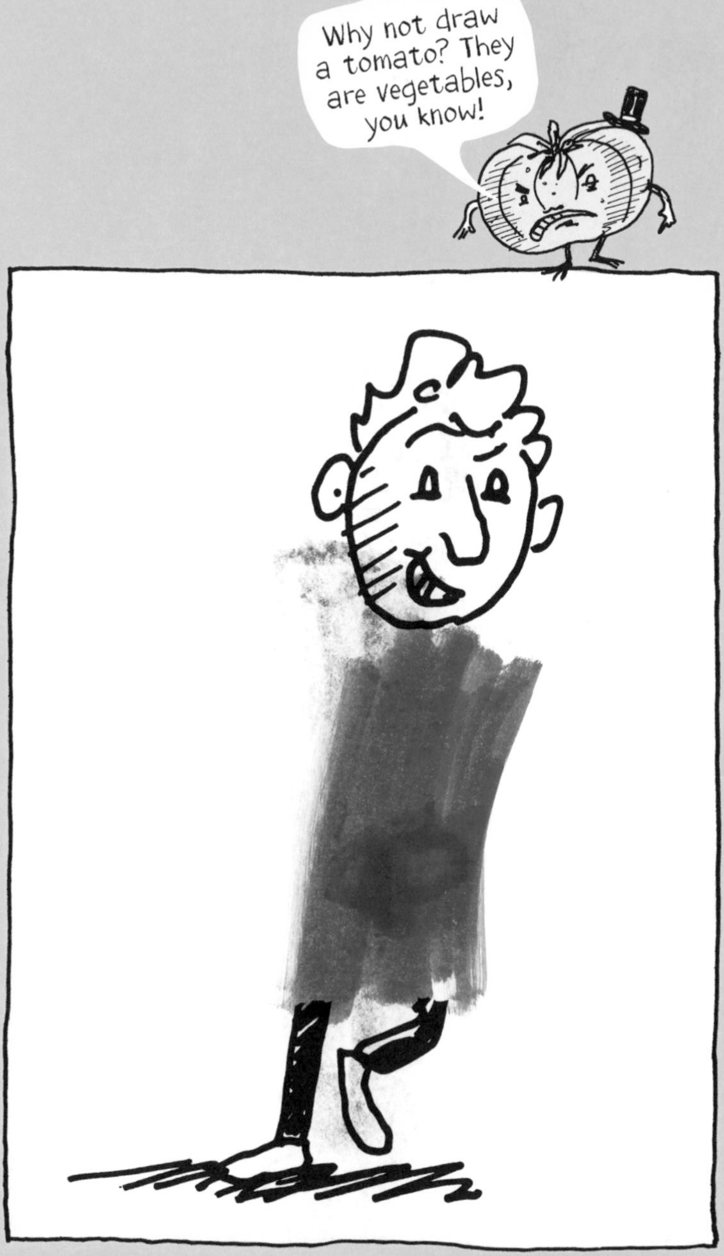
Why not draw a tomato? They are vegetables, you know!

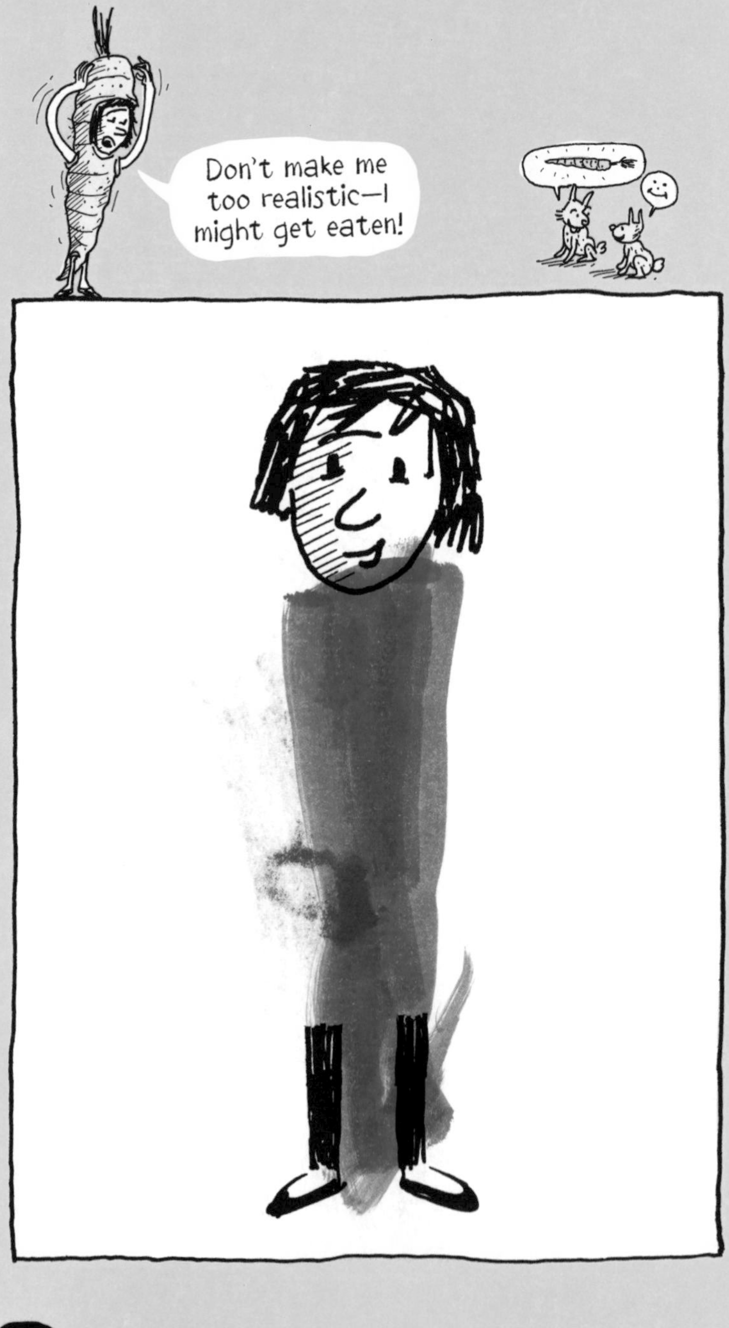
Don't make me too realistic—I might get eaten!

COLOR THIS IN . . . OR ELSE!

I need it by
5 o'clock today!

ADVERTISEMENT TIME

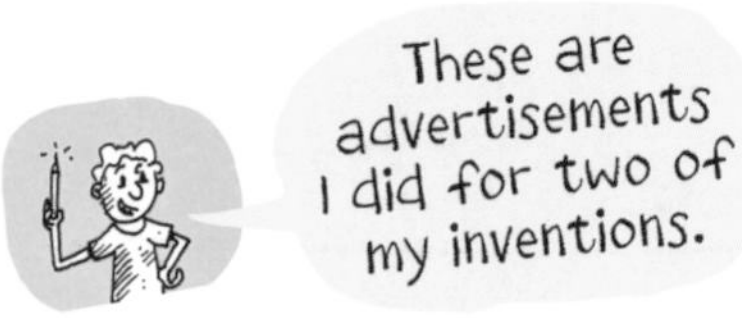
These are advertisements I did for two of my inventions.

NEW
SPOONCIL
UNBELIEVABLE
IT'S A SPOON AND A PENCIL AT THE SAME TIME!
Food
Spooncil
CHOMP CHOMP
Drawing
Child
Drawing
You can DRAW and EAT at the SAME time with SPOONCIL!
(IT REALLY WORKS)

TERRY'S MICRO-MINI MEGAPHONE
NEW
(IT REALLY WORKS)
TALKING TO GIANTS HAS NEVER BEEN SO EASY!!
ANOTHER FABULOUS TERRY INVENTION

Create your own advertisement for a product you'd like to invent.

Bed

+

tramplin

=

Bed

VAPORIZING VEGETABLES TIME

What vegetable would you like to vaporize? Draw it under the ray.

VAPORIZE!!

FEEDING TIME

Terry and I have a marshmallow machine that automatically shoots marshmallows into our mouths whenever we're hungry.

If you had a machine like this what food would you like it to feed you? Draw it.

SAFETY TIME

This is the Master Control Panel from Safety Central Headquarters.

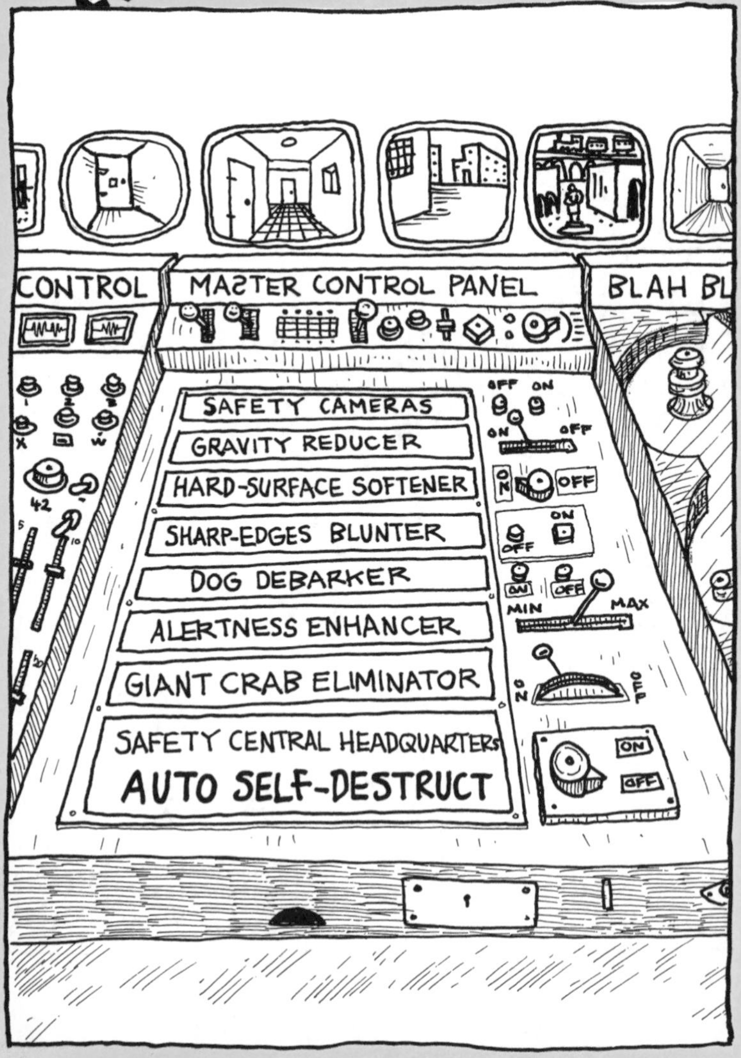
CONTROL
MASTER CONTROL PANEL
BLAH BL
SAFETY CAMERAS
GRAVITY REDUCER
HARD-SURFACE SOFTENER
SHARP-EDGES BLUNTER
DOG DEBARKER
ALERTNESS ENHANCER
GIANT CRAB ELIMINATOR
SAFETY CENTRAL HEADQUARTERS
AUTO SELF-DESTRUCT
OFF ON
ON OFF
MIN MAX

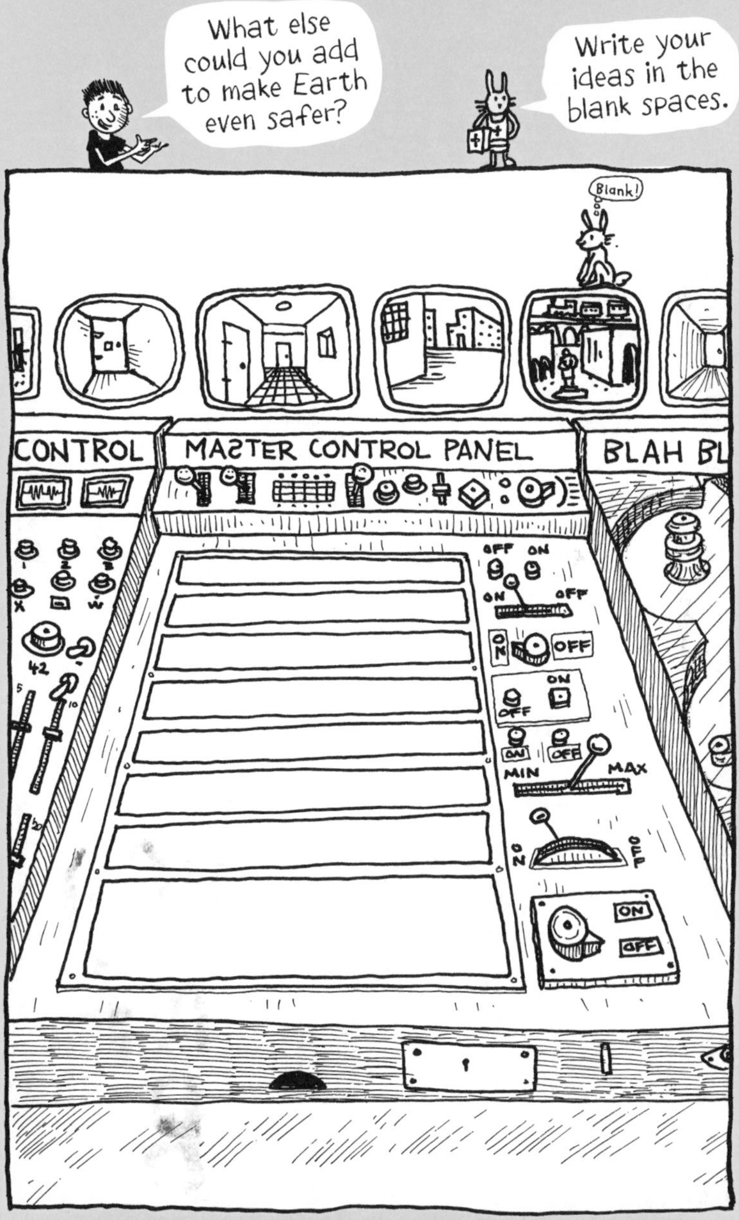
What else could you add to make Earth even safer?
Write your ideas in the blank spaces.
Blank!
CONTROL
MASTER CONTROL PANEL
BLAH BL
OFF ON
ON OFF
ON OFF
ON OFF
ON OFF
MIN MAX
ON OFF
ON OFF
42

WHAT'S CHASING ANDY?

UH-OH. Looks like Andy and Terry are being chased. But by what? You decide and then draw it.

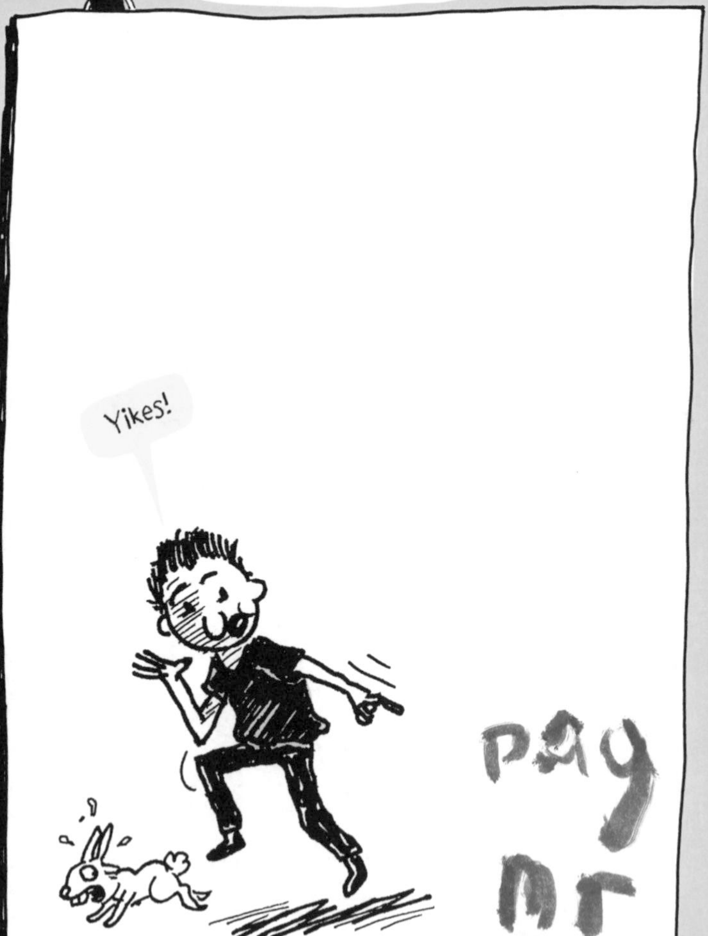
Yikes!

WHAT'S CHASING TERRY?

Yikes!
mr
B

FUN FOOD LEVEL

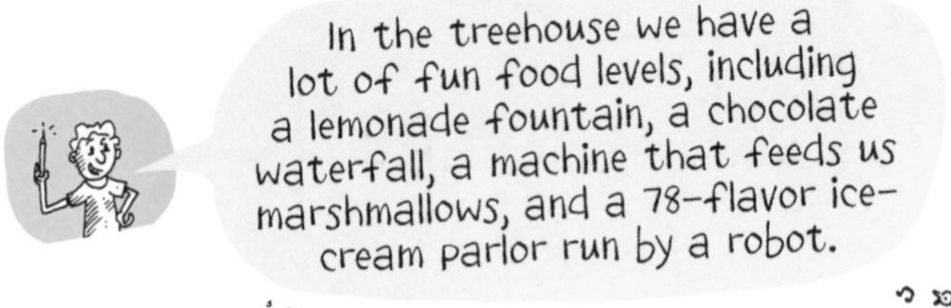
In the treehouse we have a lot of fun food levels, including a lemonade fountain, a chocolate waterfall, a machine that feeds us marshmallows, and a 78-flavor ice-cream parlor run by a robot.

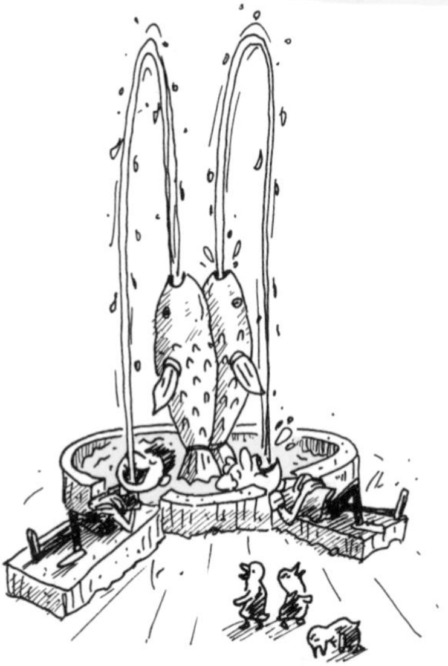

LEMONADE FOUNTAIN

NO NOT SWIMMING IN THE CHOCOLATE WATERFALL

CHOCOLATE WATERFALL

MARSHMALLOW MACHINE

Ants
choc chips
Dried slugs
sprin-kles
1000s & 1,000,000s
Pepper

ICE-CREAM PARLOR

Create your own fun food level.

STORY TIME

I like stories with lots of action.

0
2
4
6
8
16
32
64
128
256
512
1024
OFF THE SCALE
DEATH RAY
ACTION
MCVII

FRUIT-AND-VEGETABLE-BASED TRANSPORT OPTIONS
CRUISING CARROT
FLYING BEETROOT
FLOATING PEACH
HIGH-SPEED WATERMELON
SINKING STRAWBERRY
ROCKET-PROPELLED EGGPLANT
COIN RETURN
I like nonsense and random stuff.

I like animal stories. I also like stories with a little bit of romance.

1
2
3
4
5
DANGER
100
ROMANCE
USE WITH CARE

?
!

What sort of stories do you like?

I like stories with ______________________

____

____

____

____

What fish is that?

COLOR IN THE CRASH

Great picture.
It would look better in color.
You're right about that.

COLOR IN THE COVER

Color in Vegetable Patty's book cover, quick, before I eat it!
BIG NOSE BOOKS
FUN WITH VEGETABLES
by
Vegetable Patty

TREEHOUSE CODE TIME

A
B
BA
RK
C
D
Dinosaur noise.
E
F
G
H
I
J
K
L
M
N
O
P
Q
?
?
R
S
T
U
V
W
X
Y
YOU, THE READER
Z

I've used the Treehouse Code to write a message. See if you can figure out what it is.
YOU, THE READER
Dinosaur noise.
Dinosaur noise.
The answer is on page 166.

Can you use the Treehouse Code to read my message?
Dinosaur noise.
YOU, THE READER
The answer is on page 167.

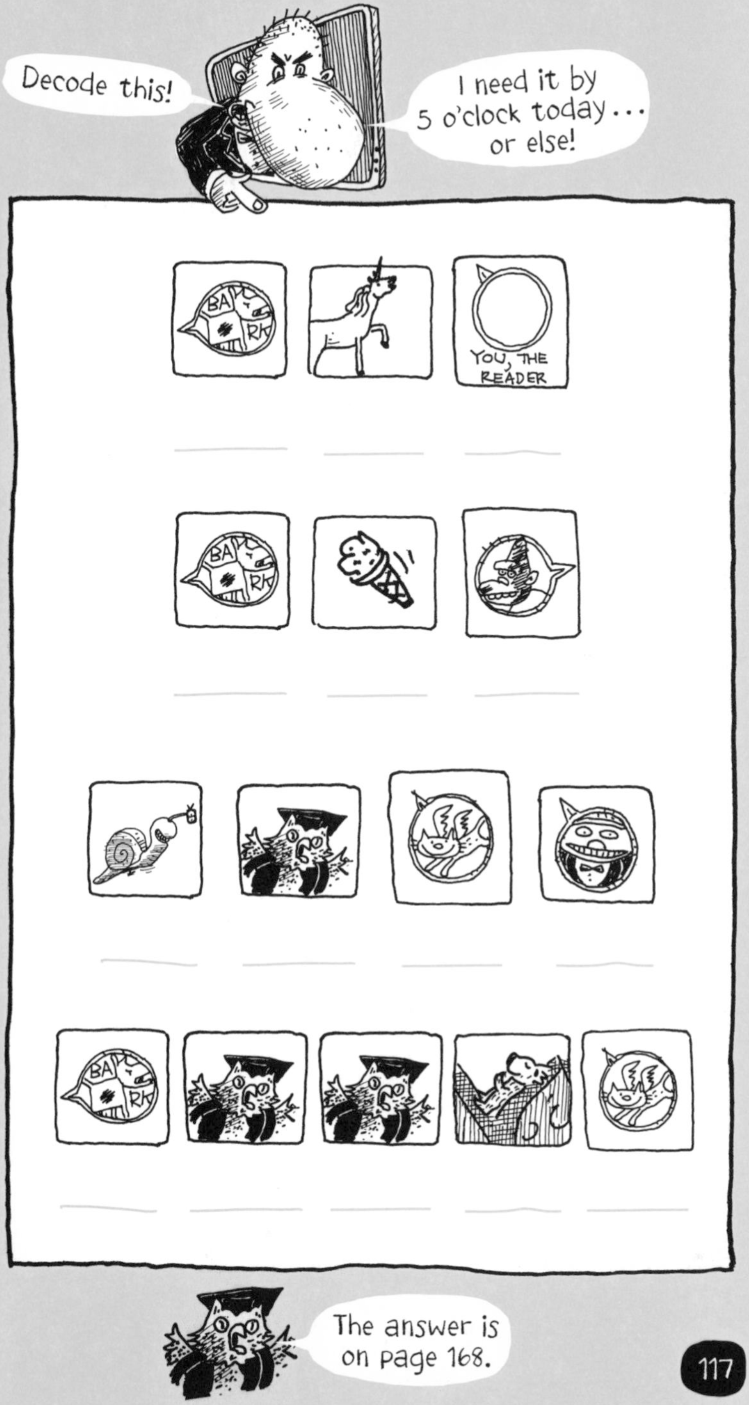
Decode this!
I need it by 5 o'clock today . . . or else!
BA
RK
YOU, THE READER
BA
RK
BA
RK
The answer is on page 168.

Can you read my message?
I hope it's about cats.
The answer is on page 169.

Superfinger says . . .

The answer is on page 170.

FIND-THE-UNICORN FUN

Too easy!
TREE-NN ANIMAL NEWS
Can you find the unicorn in each of these pictures?
NEW NEWS
MORE NEWS
BIG NEWS
OLD NEWS
GNUS
NEWS
SPARE EYEBALLS

I can't remember where I put it . . . lucky the answer is on page 171.

THE REALLY HUNGRY CATERPILLAR'S STORY

Fill in the blanks and color the pictures to tell my story.

The really hungry caterpillar

ate one _ _ _ _ _ _ _

f r i e d - _ _ _

_ _ _

_ _ _ enormous

black bird

two

_ _ _ _ _ _ _ _ _ _ _ _ _ _ _ _ _ _ _ _

______ rhinoceroses

_____ wacky waving

inflatable ____-

flailing _____ men

five giant mutant

_ _ _ _ _ _ _ _

one grumpy old

_ _ _ _ _ _

one wall of

_ _ _ _ _ _ _ _ _ _ _ _

spears

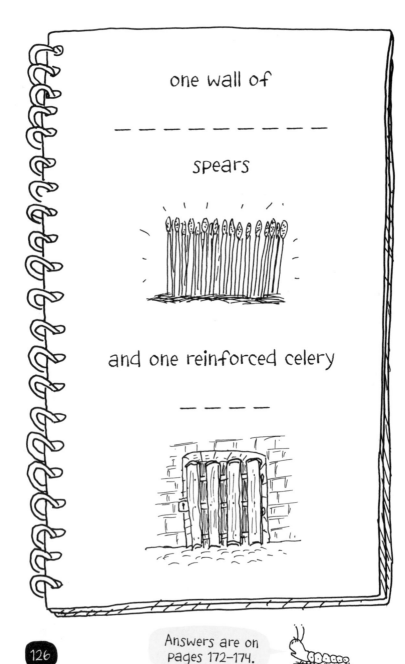

and one reinforced celery

_ _ _ _

Answers are on pages 172–174.

WHAT FAIRY TALE IS THAT?

Can you tell what stories these are?

What fish is that?

Two children, lost in the woods, find a house made of gingerbread.

H _ _ _ _ _ _

_ N _

_ _ _ _ _ _ L

While walking through the woods to Grandmother's house, a young child encounters a wolf.

L _ _ _ _ _ _

_ E _

_ _ _ _ _ _ _ G

H _ _ _

Prince Charming travels throughout his kingdom trying to find the owner of the golden slipper.

C _ _ _ _ _ _ _ L _ _ _

Answers are on page 175.

WHO REALLY SAID WHAT?!

These quotes are all mixed up. Draw a line from the speech bubble to the character who REALLY said it.

TERRY

That's crazy! SO crazy it just might work!

BARKY
THE BARKING DOG

The sharks are sick! They ate my underpants!

ANDY

BARK! BARK! BARK! BARK! BARK! BARK!

Answers are on page 176.

MR. BIG NOSE
BA-NA-NA! BA-NA-NA!

JILL
Don't argue! I'm a busy man— I don't have time to argue!

GIANT GORILLA
You went off and left me here all small.

CANNON-BLASTING TIME

Would you like to blast something out of our cannon?

3... 2... 1...
BLAM!

Draw what (or who) it is flying through the air.
You could draw your little brother...
Or, maybe, your teacher...

DINNERTIME

Dinnertime! Draw a line from each animal to its food bowl.

1001 WAYS TO COOK THISTLES

BILL & PHIL

MANNY

SILKY

Answers are on page 177.

PINK

CURLY

MR.HEE-H

LOOMPY

TRAM-RIDE TIME

Ding! Ding!

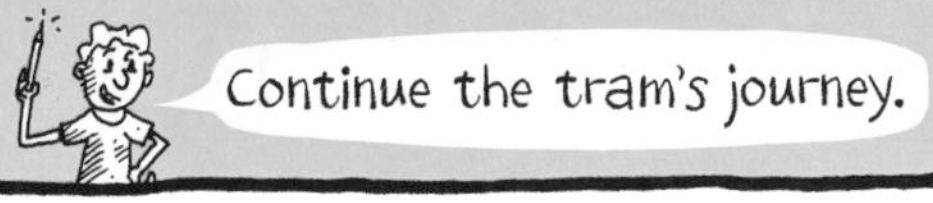
Continue the tram's journey.

FIND THE ODD ONE OUT

Can you find the odd one out?
Hint: it's something to do with where we live.
MR. HEE-HAW
PAT
SILKY, THE FLYING CAT
BABY DINOSAURS
The answer is on page 178.
MOE

TREE-COLORING TIME

Psst. Color us in too!

TREEHOUSE TRUE OR FALSE?

Mark the boxes to show if these statements are true or false.

T F

☐ ☐ 1. Silky is my favorite pet.

☐ ☐ 2. Mr. Big Nose has a very bad temper.

☐ ☐ 3. Ninja Snails move very quickly.

☐ ☐ 4. Andy and Terry live in a 13-story motor home.

☐ ☐ 5. I live in a house full of animals.

☐ ☐ 6. Andy and Terry love vegetables.

☐ ☐ 7. Bill the postman is a policeman.

☐ ☐ 8. Terry painted Silky yellow.

☐ ☐ 9. The Trunkinator is a boxing elephant.

☐ ☐ 10. Andy and Terry once worked in the monkey house at the zoo.

☐ ☐ 11. ATM stands for Automatic Tea Machine.

☐ ☐ 12. Prince Potato really likes Andy and Terry and is happy to spend time with them.

☐ ☐ 13. The treehouse has a see-through swimming pool.

Answers are on page 179.

FIND THE ODD ONE OUT

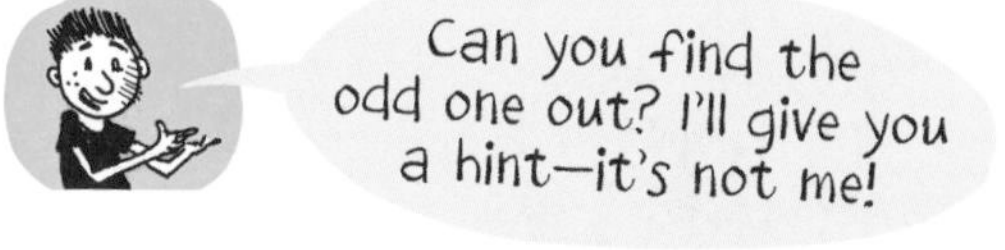
Can you find the odd one out? I'll give you a hint—it's not me!

ANDY
TERRY
EDWARD SCOOPERHANDS
MR. BIG NOSE
BILL THE POSTMAN

The answer is on page 180.

TREEHOUSE CROSSWORD

Use the clues to fill in the crossword.

ACROSS

1. He writes the words
3. He draws the pictures
7. Very wise animals that live in the treehouse
9. Short for Automatic Tattoo Machine
10. What Terry is training his snails to be
14. Andy and Terry have a Flying Fried-Egg — — —
15. He's a postman

DOWN

1. They live in the ant farm
2. Andy and Terry have a Maze of — — — —
4. Andy and Terry have a Rocking Horse — — — — — — — — —
5. The part of the Flying Fried-Egg Car that Andy and Terry sit in
6. Terry's second favorite TV show is *Buzzy the Buzzing* — — —
8. What Andy wants to do in every contest
11. Andy and Terry's neighbor and friend
12. Jill's pet cat
13. What Terry and Andy live in

Answers are on page 181.

CROSSWORD!
CLUES!
POOP-POOP!

1
2
3
4
5
6
7
8
9
10
11
12
13
14
15

DRAW ANDY IN DANGER

I love drawing pictures of Andy in terrible danger. Help me finish these ones by drawing over the lines in the pictures of the dangerous animals.

I can't watch this.
Me neither!

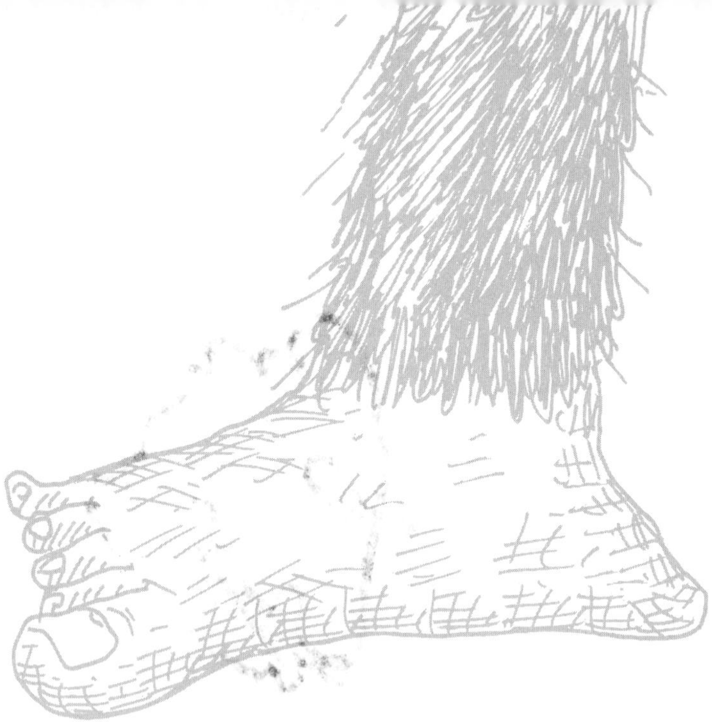

Be quie
Barky, I'
trying t
read.
BARK!

That's weird
...I can smell
elephant.

Dinnertime!

CATAPULT FUN

What would you like to get rid of? Draw it in our giant catapult.
Bye!
SPROING!

ANTIGRAVITY TIME

All this writing, drawing and puzzle solving has been fun, but I'm exhausted.
Me too. Let's go for a nice, relaxing float in the antigravity chamber.
But I'm too tired to draw us in there.
Why don't we ask the readers to do it?
Great idea, Jill!
Z
Z
ZZZ

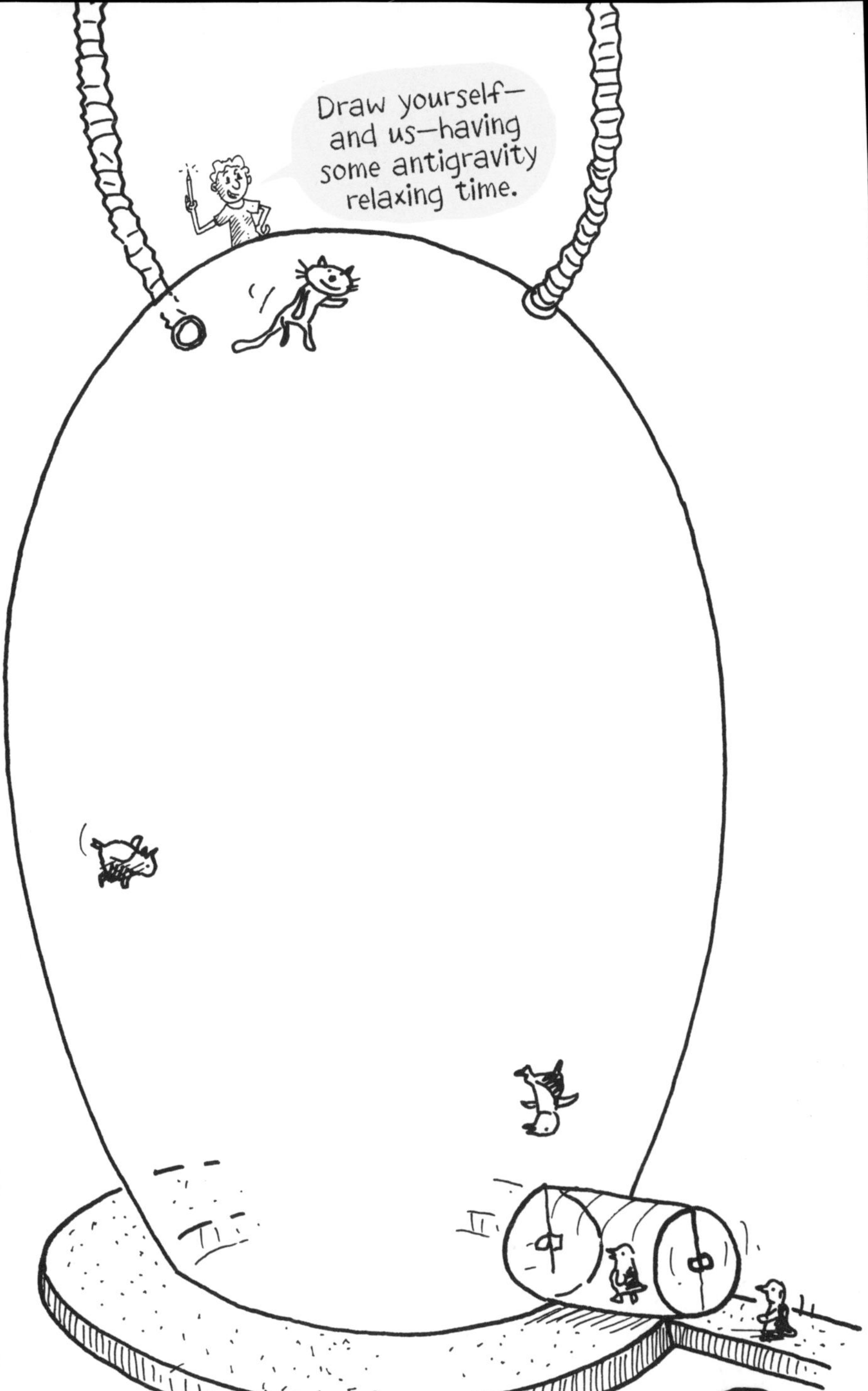
Draw yourself—
and us—having
some antigravity
relaxing time.

ANSWER TIME

SPOT THE DIFFERENCE (PAGES 32–33)

SPOT THE DIFFERENCE (PAGES 42–43)

Mommy, those two don't look like real monkeys.
Shhh! Don't talk so loud. You'll hurt their feelings.
Shut up and eat.
I love bananas.

ESCAPE THE MAZE OF DOOM (PAGE 46)

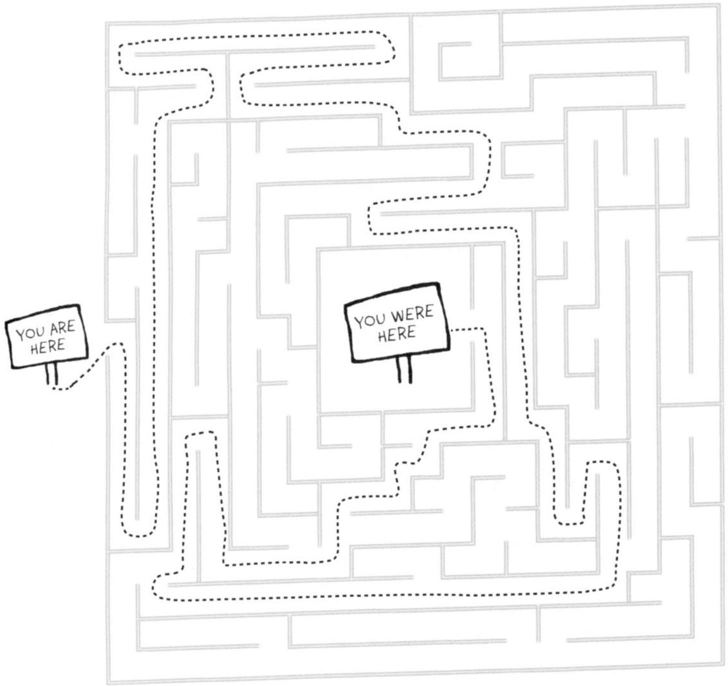
YOU ARE HERE
YOU WERE HERE

13-STORY TREEHOUSE WORD SEARCH (PAGE 48)

S	E	A	M	O	N	K	E	Y	S
C	G	A	N	A	N	A	B	R	W
A	N	S	M	O	O	B	N	O	I
T	I	N	G	K	I	A	V	T	N
A	L	E	S	G	S	T	I	A	G
P	W	H	W	E	E	H	N	R	I
U	O	C	A	Y	M	R	E	O	N
L	B	T	P	A	D	O	S	B	G
T	N	I	C	H	A	O	S	A	E
Y	E	K	N	O	M	M	S	L	S

Solution: MONKEY MADNESS

26-STORY TREEHOUSE WORD SEARCH (PAGE 54)

W	O	O	D	E	N	H	E	A	D
I	T	O	I	D	U	T	S	L	U
C	A	L	O	O	P	C	N	O	M
E	T	S	L	L	U	A	R	Z	U
C	T	E	S	U	C	P	H	N	D
R	O	T	K	E	B	T	Y	O	F
E	O	A	A	Z	K	U	M	G	I
A	Y	R	T	A	P	R	E	R	G
M	I	I	E	M	R	E	A	O	H
T	S	P	L	A	T	D	E	G	T

Solution: UNLUCKY PIRATE

Eeeee-yaahhhhhhhhh!

39-STORY TREEHOUSE WORD SEARCH (PAGE 61)

T	R	A	M	P	O	L	I	N	E
W	E	T	A	L	O	C	O	H	C
A	V	T	O	O	R	T	E	E	B
T	O	S	P	O	O	N	C	I	L
E	L	M	S	L	A	P	A	Y	R
R	C	O	S	L	A	P	N	K	O
F	A	O	S	L	A	P	D	L	C
A	N	N	T	E	R	R	Y	I	K
L	O	D	I	P	U	T	S	S	E
L	U	N	I	N	V	E	N	T	T

Solution: SLAP! SLAP! SLAP!

SLAP!
SLAP!

SPOT THE DIFFERENCE (PAGES 64–65)

BARKY, THE BARKING DOG
AT THE BEACH

TREEHOUSE TRIVIA (PAGE 71)

1. What is the name of the sea monster Terry fell in love with?

   Mermaidia

2. What is the worst job Andy and Terry ever had?

   Filling in for the monkeys at the zoo

3. What is Terry's favorite TV show?

   The Barky the Barking Dog Show

4. What color did Terry paint Silky?

   Yellow

5. What is the name of Andy and Terry's publisher?

   Mr. Big Nose

6. What is the name of the pirate who captured Andy, Terry, and me?

   Captain Woodenhead

7. How many flavors of ice cream are there in Edward Scooperhands' ice-cream parlor?

   78

SPOT THE DIFFERENCE (PAGES 74–75)

THE BIG FAT COW THAT GOES KAPOW!
Z
Z
Z

52-STORY TREEHOUSE WORD SEARCH (PAGE 76)

D	E	T	E	C	T	I	V	E	S
E	P	E	C	N	I	R	P	Y	E
G	O	N	B	I	G	D	A	L	R
G	T	S	O	T	V	I	P	F	E
P	A	N	N	S	E	S	A	R	M
L	T	A	I	Y	E	G	T	E	E
A	O	I	N	D	G	U	T	T	M
N	E	L	J	N	T	I	Y	T	B
T	A	S	A	A	B	S	L	U	E
E	T	E	R	R	Y	E	S	B	R

Solution: EAT VEGETABLES

VEGETABLE PATTY SAYS:
EAT YOUR VEGETABLES!

SPOT THE DIFFERENCE (PAGES 86–87)

10°
FRUIT-AND-VEGETABLE-BASED TRANSPORT OPTIONS
CRUISING CARROT
FLYING BEETROOT
FLOATING PEACH
HIGH-SPEED WATERMELON
ROCKET-PROPELLED EGGPLANT
SINKING STRAWBERRY
COIN RETURN

ANIMAL SCRAMBLES (PAGES 90–91)

RM EEH WAH

MR. HEE HAW

EMO

MOE

SLIYK

SILKY

LRARY

LARRY

BLLI & PILH

BILL & PHIL

TAP

PAT

65-STORY TREEHOUSE WORD SEARCH (PAGE 93)

B	G	S	B	T	P	Y	G	E	L
U	N	U	A	S	B	I	N	P	E
B	I	P	R	N	E	R	I	F	V
B	N	E	C	O	T	L	O	P	A
L	O	R	P	S	O	S	F	O	R
E	L	B	L	P	E	R	M	I	T
W	C	W	T	R	E	E	N	N	E
R	O	T	C	E	P	S	N	I	M
A	S	P	S	S	P	M	A	R	I
P	O	N	D	S	C	U	M	P	T

Solution: POOP-POOP

CHICKEN!
CHUTNEY!
POOP-POOP!

FIND THE ODD ONE OUT (PAGE 94)

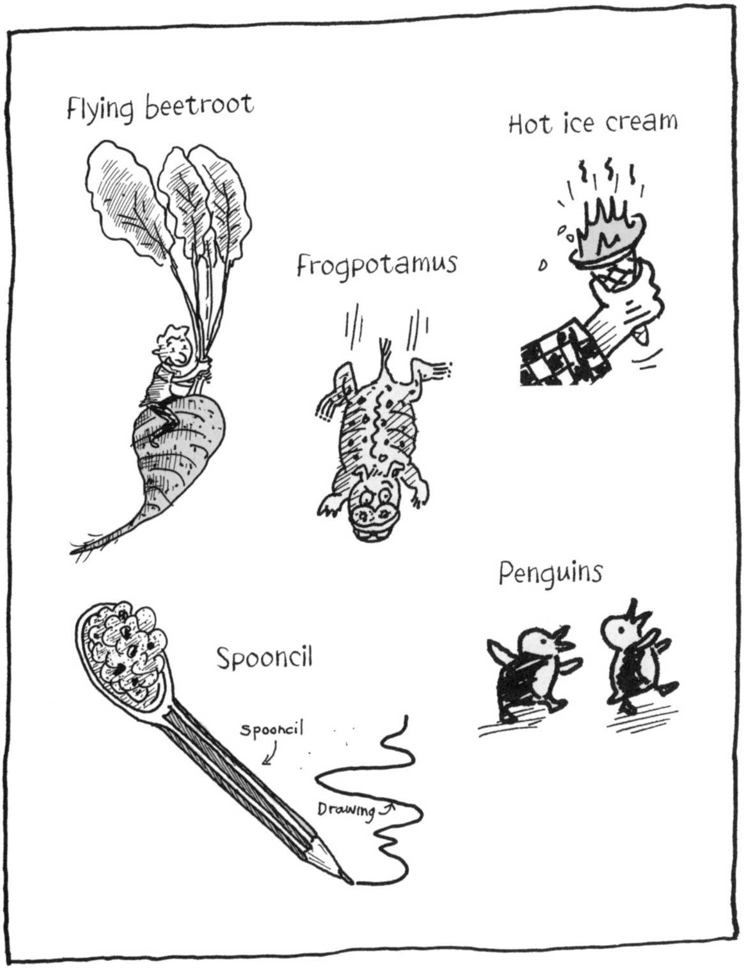

Flying beetroot
Hot ice cream
Frogpotamus
Penguins
Spooncil
Spooncil
Drawing

Answer: Spooncil.

It's the only one Professor Stupido didn't un-invent.

TREEHOUSE CODE TIME (PAGE 115)

YOU, THE READER
T E R R Y
I S A
Dinosaur noise.
D U M
Dinosaur noise.
D U M

TREEHOUSE CODE TIME (PAGE 116)

Dinosaur noise.
YOU, THE READER
A N D Y
C A N' T
C O U N T

TREEHOUSE CODE TIME (PAGE 117)

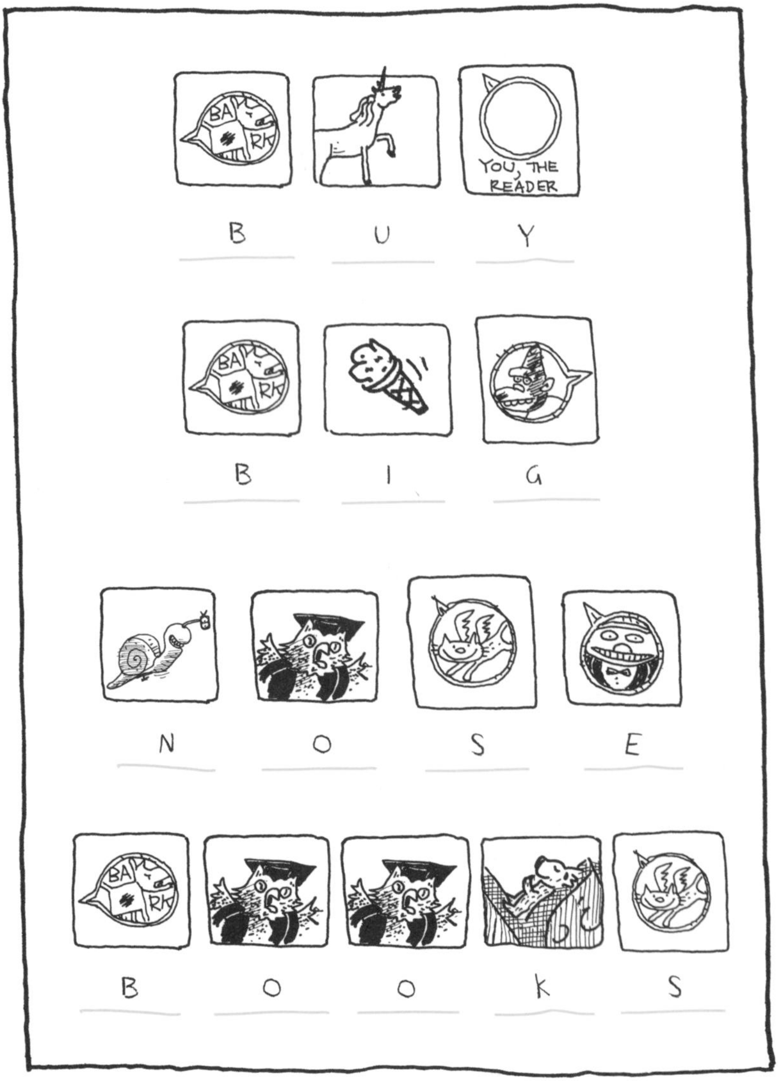
YOU, THE READER
B U Y
B I G
N O S E
B O O K S

TREEHOUSE CODE TIME (PAGE 118)

I
L O V E
C A T S
YAY!

TREEHOUSE CODE TIME (PAGE 119)

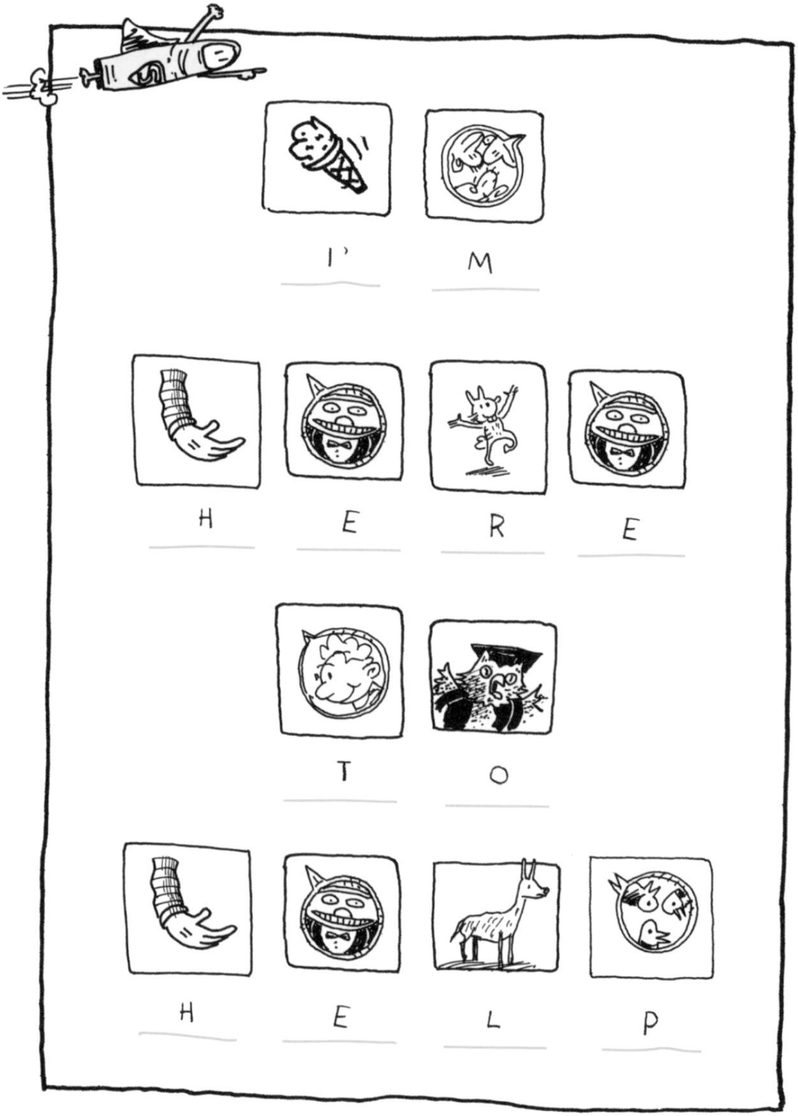

I'
M
H
E
R
E
T
O
H
E
L
P

FIND-THE-UNICORN FUN (PAGES 120–121)

REE-NN
ANIMAL NEWS
Can you find the unicorn in each of these pictures?
NEW NEWS
MORE NEWS
BIG NEWS
OLD NEWS
GNUS
NEWS
SPARE EYEBALLS

PAGE 122

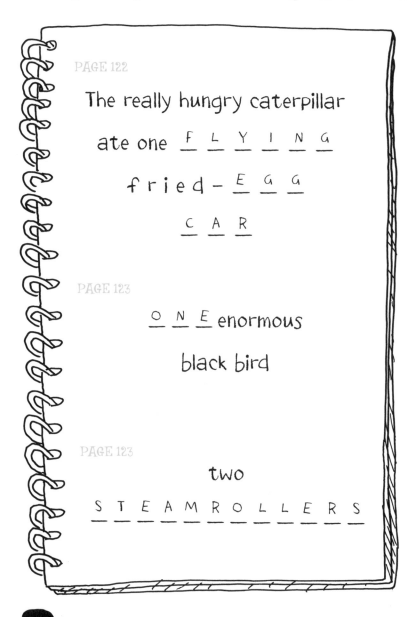

The really hungry caterpillar

ate one F L Y I N G

fried-E G G

C A R

PAGE 123

O N E enormous

black bird

PAGE 123

two

S T E A M R O L L E R S

PAGE 124

T H R E E rhinoceroses

PAGE 124

F O U R wacky waving inflatable A R M - flailing T U B E men

PAGE 125

five giant mutant S P I D E R S

PAGE 125

one grumpy old

T O M A T O

PAGE 126

one wall of

A S P A R A G U S

spears

PAGE 126

and one reinforced celery

D O O R

WHAT FAIRY TALE IS THAT? (PAGES 127–129)

PAGE 127

HANSEL AND GRETEL

PAGE 128

LITTLE RED RIDING HOOD

PAGE 129

CINDERELLA

WHO REALLY SAID WHAT?! (PAGES 130–131)

TERRY

The sharks are sick! They ate my underpants!

BA
RK
BARKY THE BARKING DOG

BARK! BARK! BARK! BARK! BARK! BARK!

ANDY

That's crazy! SO crazy it just might work!

MR. BIG NOSE

Don't argue! I'm a busy man— I don't have time to argue!

JILL

You went off and left me here all small.

GIANT GORILLA

BA-NA-NA! BA-NA-NA!

DINNERTIME (PAGES 134–135)

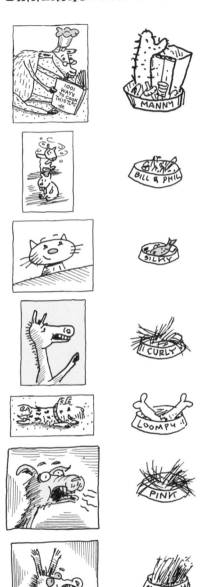

1001 WAYS TO COOK THISTLES

MANNY

BILL & PHIL

SILKY

CURLY

LOOMPY

PINK

MR.HEE-HA

FIND THE ODD ONE OUT (PAGE 138)

Answer: The baby dinosaurs are the odd ones out. They live in the treehouse, but all the other animals live at Jill's house.

MR. HEE-HAW
PAT
SILKY, THE FLYING CAT
BABY DINOSAURS
MOE

TREEHOUSE TRUE OR FALSE? (PAGE 140)

T	F	
☑	☐	1. Silky is my favorite pet.
☑	☐	2. Mr. Big Nose has a very bad temper.
☐	☑	3. Ninja Snails move very quickly.
☐	☑	4. Andy and Terry live in a 13-story motor home.
☑	☐	5. I live in a house full of animals.
☐	☑	6. Andy and Terry love vegetables.
☐	☑	7. Bill the postman is a policeman.
☑	☐	8. Terry painted Silky yellow.
☑	☐	9. The Trunkinator is a boxing elephant.
☑	☐	10. Andy and Terry once worked in the monkey house at the zoo.
☐	☑	11. ATM stands for Automatic Tea Machine.
☐	☑	12. Prince Potato really likes Andy and Terry and is happy to spend time with them.
☑	☐	13. The treehouse has a see-through swimming pool.

FIND THE ODD ONE OUT (PAGE 141)

Answer: Edward Scooperhands is the odd one out. He is a robot, but all the others are human beings.

ANDY
TERRY
EDWARD SCOOPERHANDS
MR. BIGNOSE
BILL THE POSTMAN

TREEHOUSE CROSSWORD (PAGES 142–143)

A	N	D	Y		T	E	R	R	Y
N		O		F			A		O
T		O	W	L	S		C		L
S		M		Y			E		K
	W					A	T	M	
N	I	N	J	A	S		R		
	N		I		I		A		T
			L		L		C	A	R
B	I	L	L		K		K		E
					Y				E

Bye!
See ya later!
Till next time!
Hasta la vista, baby!

Andy Griffiths lives in an amazing treehouse with his friend Terry and together they make funny books, just like the one you're holding in your hands right now. Andy writes the words and Terry draws the pictures. If you'd like to know more, read the Treehouse series (or visit www.andygriffiths.com.au).

Terry Denton lives in an amazing treehouse with his friend Andy and together they make funny books, just like the one you're holding in your hands right now. Terry draws the pictures and Andy writes the words. If you'd like to know more, read the Treehouse series (or visit www.terrydenton.com).

Jill Griffiths lives near Andy and Terry in a house full of animals. She has two dogs, one goat, three horses, four goldfish, one cow, two guinea pigs, one camel, one donkey, thirteen cats, and so many rabbits she has lost count. If you'd like to know more, read the Treehouse series.

Thank you for reading this FEIWEL AND FRIENDS book.
The Friends who made

THE TREEHOUSE FUN BOOK

possible are:

Jean Feiwel, Publisher
Liz Szabla, Editor in Chief
Rich Deas, Senior Creative Director
Holly West, Editor
Dave Barrett, Executive Managing Editor
Kim Waymer, Production Manager
Anna Roberto, Editor
Christine Barcellona, Associate Editor
Emily Settle, Administrative Assistant
Anna Poon, Editorial Assistant

Follow us on Facebook or visit us online at mackids.com.
Our books are friends for life